HAND[...]
DR[...]

BY
MARGARET O'NEILL

MILLS & BOON LIMITED
ETON HOUSE 18–24 PARADISE ROAD
RICHMOND SURREY TW9 1SR

All the characters in this book have no existence outside the imagination of the Author, and have no relation whatsoever to anyone bearing the same name or names. They are not even distantly inspired by any individual known or unknown to the Author, and all the incidents are pure invention.

All Rights Reserved. The text of this publication or any part thereof may not be reproduced or transmitted in any form or by any means, electronic or mechanical, including photocopying, recording, storage in an information retrieval system, or otherwise, without the written permission of the publisher.

This book is sold subject to the condition that it shall not, by way of trade or otherwise, be lent, resold, hired out or otherwise circulated without the prior consent of the publisher in any form of binding or cover other than that in which it is published and without a similar condition including this condition being imposed on the subsequent purchaser.

*First published in Great Britain 1993
by Mills & Boon Limited*

© Margaret O'Neill 1993

*Australian copyright 1993
Philippine copyright 1993
This edition 1993*

ISBN 0 263 78139 9

0263 781 399 3644

*Set in 10 on 11 pt Linotron Times
03-9306-58357*

*Typeset in Great Britain by Centracet, Cambridge
Made and printed in Great Britain*

CHAPTER ONE

Lucy stared across the wide desk at Mr de Winter, the junior partner in the firm of solicitors, de Winter, Fraser, Formby and de Winter.

'The Frobishers?' Her voice was almost squeaky with surprise and disbelief. 'But I don't understand. I hardly know them—why should they have left me their property in their wills?'

Patiently, Mr de Winter went over the details again.

'Mr and Mrs Frobisher,' he said, 'apparently knew your parents well at one time, although you may not remember this.'

'Oh, yes, I do, in a vague sort of way. I saw a lot of them until I was about nine, I think, and then they quarrelled with my parents, and it was only a few months ago that I met up with them again.' Lucy was beginning to recover somewhat from the shock of learning that Mr and Mrs Frobisher were dead, killed in a road accident, and that they'd left her property, and a great deal of money.

Clive de Winter smiled at her, thinking what a delightful little girl she must have been, with her brown hair, now shoulder-length and elegantly cut, perhaps then in pigtails. And those beautiful hazel-green eyes, looking hurt and puzzled as she tried to come to terms with the Frobishers' sudden deaths and her unexpected windfall.

'You ask why they left you a large part of their estate, Miss Shaw. I can only tell you that they altered their wills a short while ago, and I know that it was after meeting you again when Mrs Frobisher was in hospital and you nursed her. That much they told me.

But you'd always been in their wills, although not as the main beneficiary, and not as the inheritor of the school. The wills are sound, incontestable. The Frobishers apparently never forgot their close friendship with your parents, and they never forgot you.'

'But suppose they have relatives who feel they should have something? It seems only fair. My parents used to say blood was thicker than water, and charity begins at home, and though they may sound only clichés, I rather believe in them myself.'

Mr de Winter remained patient. It was, after all, his job, but in this case a pleasure too; one didn't often get tall, slim, brown-haired, green-eyed beauties in the office. The idea popped into his mind that she must look stunning in her nurse's uniform, and, according to the Frobishers, she was a wonderful nurse—competent, compassionate and caring, they had said. The sort of qualities they had looked for in the staff of their school, as Clive, who had been their friend as well as their solicitor, knew.

'Well, there aren't any relatives, that's certainly one reason why they were so attached to you and your parents, and I know from what they told me that they were devastated by the break-up of their friendship. I understand they tried to make contact with you when your parents died about a year ago.'

'Yes, they died within a few weeks of each other, my mother from cancer and my father from a heart attack.' Lucy blinked back tears. 'The Frobishers wrote, they wanted to come to the funerals, but I asked them not to. It would have somehow seemed like a betrayal of my parents. Ridiculous really, I have no idea what the original quarrel was about, but it had certainly spoilt four people's lives—five, if you count me.'

'You were affected by what happened, then, although you were young?'

'I remember missing them at the time in a vague sort

of way, but it was when I nursed Mrs Frobisher a few months ago that I realised what nice people they were, and thought how sad it was that things had happened the way that they had. And now they're dead too, and no relatives of their own to miss them.'

Clive de Winter thought, Lucky old Frobishers, to have this stunning girl grieve for them. I wonder why they didn't try harder to make it up with the Shaws, or was it the Shaws who remained implacable? Well, that was a puzzle that would never be solved now that the nice old couple were dead and gone. But he was delighted for Miss Shaw that the Frobishers had chosen her as their heir. It was rash of a solicitor to form opinions based on instinct rather than fact, but on this occasion he felt justified. The young woman before him, he was convinced, was good as well as beautiful, and as a bonus, intelligent.

He had no idea what her circumstances were or if her parents had left her anything. As a nurse she probably wasn't well off; she was too young to hold a very senior post. The nice little fortune that had been left to her must surely be a godsend.

'I don't know that I should accept this—this gift, or whatever you call it,' said Lucy.

Her words jolted Clive de Winter out of his reverie. 'But you can't turn it down, Miss Shaw—it's ridiculous.' He recovered himself. 'I'm sorry, that's not for me to say, of course. What you do with your inheritance is your own affair, once you have it. But I do beg you to think it over carefully, not come to any rash decisions, give yourself a little time. Do remember that these kind people, the Frobishers, wanted you to have their school. They wanted you to take care of it in their memory, and the school was their life.'

Lucy's lovely mouth, a little wide perhaps for classical beauty, trembled at the corners. She lowered her head for a moment, and when she raised it again, her eyes were very bright as if with unshed tears, but she was smiling.

'How long have I got to think about it?' Her voice was low and slightly husky.

'Oh, plenty of time; we legal beavers are a slow-moving lot. There are many formalities to go through yet. You probably have commitments. . .?'

He let his voice trail off, hoping for a reply that might give him a clue about his new client. He wasn't a particularly imaginative man, but he was kind and used to dealing with people in receipt of bad, or — as in this case — mixed news, and they all suffered shock to a certain degree. If he could find out a little more about Miss Shaw, other than that she was living in a bedsit in Islington and seemed to be totally lacking close relatives, he might be better able to advise her.

She gave a funny little laugh. 'No, no commitments. In fact. . .'

Clive de Winter began to see daylight. This delightful young woman as a young nurse was probably hard up, as most of those working in the health field were. If her parents hadn't left her anything much, and they might have used up savings and pensions during long illnesses, she could probably do with some cash immediately.

He said, deliberately keeping his voice cool, professional, picking his words with care, 'If you need an advance against your inheritance, this can be arranged without difficulty. It's quite a normal procedure.' He smiled to reassure her, and let her see that he was not handing out charity. 'Of course, it would be treated like a normal loan, with interest charged and so on. Would that help? You'll have ample funds to discharge it when probate and so on is resolved.'

A whole variety of emotions chased themselves across the flower-like face in front of him. Lucy said at last, in a low voice, 'It's not my money really, I'm used to living a sort of hand-to-mouth existence.' She smiled across at him. 'Most agency nurses are, you know. The money's quite good when one is working, but non-existent when one isn't, and these days, with cutbacks and so on, this happens, even in nursing. I'm used to signing on between jobs. Well, not recently, because I was looking after my parents, and I was at home for a while.'

She was quite naturally shattered by the death of her parents. The solicitor knew nothing of the details of their passing except for what she had just told him, that she had for a while nursed them at home. If they had a home, why, soon after they died, had she moved into a bedsitting-room?

He was horrified to think that this charming young woman might have to 'sign on', as she had put it so nonchalantly, especially with a small fortune and a flourishing business awaiting her. He must try to make her see reason.

'Miss Shaw,' he smiled at her across the desk, 'may I, as a friend as well as solicitor to the late André and Jeanette Frobisher, and, I hope, a friend to you, suggest that you accept something from the estate whatever you eventually decide to do with it? This will give you time to think rationally and make a balanced decision.'

She said in a rush, 'It's not money so much — I've explained, I could get by and I've a little saved and something from the sale of the house, though my father had remortgaged it to pay for some private treatment for my mother, so there wasn't a lot left. My problem is that I'd been accepted for a post with the Wessex Health Authority, with living accommodation, and now they say that they can't employ me. It was a newly created post, you see, as a nurse therapist, because I had some drama training before I started nursing.'

'I see,' he said, though he didn't really understand.

'I have to get out of my bedsit in a few weeks' time, but then I thought I——'

He broke in, appalled, 'Would have somewhere to live, and now you haven't?'

'Yes.' She gave him a half-smile of resignation. He was about to speak when the internal phone buzzed. With a murmured apology, he picked up the receiver. 'Yes—no,' he said, and gave Lucy a smile. 'Show her in.' He turned to Lucy. 'I have another client to see, rather a difficult lady; can't keep her waiting longer. Can you come back at five-thirty?'

'Oh, yes, of course.'

'I think I have an idea,' said Clive de Winter. 'But I must consult with my father. He's joint executor to the Frobishers' will.'

Lucy gathered up her shoulder-bag, gloves and umbrella. 'Thank you,' she said in her husky voice. 'You've been very kind.'

'Not at all. I hope we can resolve your problems. Please don't worry.'

'I won't.'

She passed an irate-looking horsey sort of woman in the waiting-room, and smiled. 'I'm so sorry,' she said. 'If you're waiting to see Mr Clive de Winter, it's my fault that he's behind with his appointments.'

The severe, tweedy, loud-voiced lady returned her smile. 'It's all right, m'dear, not to worry.'

'You're very kind.'

'Not at all.' The lady beamed at Lucy and stalked towards Clive de Winter's office. 'He's very sound, y'know, young Clive, like his father.

Clive de Winter, not so young, in his late thirties, standing in the doorway ready to placate Mrs Marjory Brand, steadied himself against the door-jamb. Never had he heard the redoubtable and very rich Mrs Brand sound so cordial, never had she complimented him, as far as he knew. It just shows, he reflected, how youth, beauty and goodness can affect us all.

Lucy, with a smile and a thank-you to the receptionist, passed out into the vestibule, and leaned against the wall beside the office door. I must pull myself together, she thought, and be sensible, while I kill time before I see Mr de Winter later.

Rain was beating hard against the windows on either side of the massive front door. She paused to belt her tan silk mackintosh round her slender waist. Her usual nimble fingers were all thumbs, and her mind was in a turmoil of excitement and apprehension. She felt almost faint. She began to unfurl her long elegant umbrella as she walked across the vestibule, and because her feet were at that moment as clumsy as her hands, she tripped.

The front door was opened and she stumbled into a large, rock-like person, who stopped her in her tracks.

'Steady,' rumbled a deep male voice, and a strong hand supported her elbow. The voice was extraordinarily gravelly, and the grey, curiously flecked eyes, which she met as she raised her head with a defiant toss, seemed to match the voice. They were deep, fathomless.

Lucy was cross with herself for being so fanciful and for tripping up. She wasn't usually so clumsy.

'Thank you,' she said politely in her soft, husky voice.

The very masculine, large person before her frowned, then growled something unintelligible.

Her actress's eye, which, in spite of years of nursing, she hadn't lost, absorbed his main physical attributes at a glance. Real leading-man material. Many leading men were short or barely average height, which was why being a tall, willowy beauty didn't automatically set one up as a female star performer. What leading man wanted to be looked down on by his female costar? No one that Lucy could think of. Not that this man would care a jot — he wouldn't need to.

He was tall, six feet plus, broad-shouldered, narrow-hipped and muscular. He was wearing a white, faintly military-looking raincoat that emphasised his athletic physique. His face was handsome in a lean, lined fasion, with a strong aquiline nose, formidable chin and thick, well marked eyebrows. His hair, black, liberally speckled with grey, swept back from a pronounced widow's peak, gave him a faintly mephistophelean look. He was too sure of himself by half, and represented virtually everything that Lucy distrusted in a man.

'Thank you,' she repeated, and gently shook his hand from her arm. 'I'm quite capable of looking after myself.'

She moved away, and immediately tripped over the snow-whitened step in front of the porticoed doorway. The large man grasped her arm and stopped her from falling.

He smiled sarcastically, and Lucy gritted her teeth. 'Oh, quite, I can see that.' He peered at her closely, questioningly, and seemed to reach a conclusion. 'You've had a shock,' he said. 'Go and get a sweet drink and take it easy for a moment.'

'That,' she replied, icily correct, 'is what I intend to do.'

'Good.'

She was conscious, as she left the solicitors' offices, that the stranger was watching her as she made her way down the tail end of the High Street to Market Square, which she crossed to enter The Copper Kettle tea-rooms.

He was still watching, she noticed, as she shook off her wet umbrella in the doorway, but he had disappeared before she actually entered the tea-rooms, into the solicitors' office.

The Copper Kettle was warm, aromatic and friendly. Lucy ordered fresh tea-cakes, for which the café was locally famous, and Earl Grey tea with lemon. In deference to the stranger's suggestion and her own common sense, she added, against her normal taste, sugar to her cup.

She drained her third cup, and was enjoying her second enormous toasted tea-cake, oozing with butter, when the shop door opened to a clang from the old-fashioned bell, and the tall stranger entered. He spent a few moments shaking off his spiked, no-nonsense, large black umbrella before backing into the room.

There were no empty tables. Lucy saw him looking around. His eye lighted on her.

He stalked over to her table. 'Do you mind?' he asked.

She wondered, as she shook her head and waved a hand towards the empty chair, what he would have said or done had she indicated otherwise. Not a lot, she thought. He certainly wouldn't have been embarrassed. He probably knew from experience that any woman in her right mind would be delighted to share a table with him.

'Please,' she said, deliberately gracious.

'Thank you.' He gave her a smile that made her stomach churn. His mouth said it was only for her, and yet his eyes remained cool, distant, arctic grey.

'Will you join me?' he asked.

His voice was expressionless, yet she felt it would have been churlish to refuse. 'I'll have some more tea, please.'

'Earl Grey with lemon?'

Lucy nodded.

He ordered, with toasted tea-cakes for himself.

'Nice place,' he said, glancing round the steamy room.

'Yes, unspoilt in spite of its name.'

He gave a wolfish grin. 'A commercial necessity, probably.'

'Probably.'

His tea and toasted tea-cakes arrived. He poured Lucy another cup and added a slice of lemon with the silvered tongs from the glass dish. Then he poured his own tea and carefully buttered a tea-cake, cut it into pieces, forked up a portion and popped it neatly into his mouth, scrunching contentedly. For a large man his movements were very neat and contained, Lucy thought.

He wiped his mouth with the paper napkin provided. 'Scrumptious,' he said. It sounded odd coming from him, almost too fulsome.

'Yes, they are delicious—I've had two.'

'You needed them.'

'Yes.'

He munched away for a few moments, cleared his mouth, and produced a wintry smile. 'Got over your fright, or shock, or whatever?' he asked.

Irrationally, Lucy was tempted to be angry or at least irritated with him, but the need to talk to someone, even a complete stranger, prevented her. And the way he had asked seemed not in the least offensive, perhaps because it was so impersonal.

'Yes, I feel much better, thank you.'

'Good.'

The very fact that he seemed incurious made her want to tell him what the solicitor had told her. For some reason that she couldn't fathom, he seemed the sort of person in whom one could confide. How ridiculous. He was a cold fish.

'Are you visiting Chelchester?' she asked for something to say.

'At the moment, yes.' He smiled again. His grey eyes bored into her. 'And you—are you visiting?'

She wanted to pour it all out, about the inheritance,

her uncertainty, the strange fact that this morning she had nothing, and now she had, could have, everything. The ingrained habit of a lifetime helped. One couldn't pour out one's troubles to a stranger.

'I too,' she replied, well in control, 'am only visiting at present.'

'Ah, for some reason I thought you knew the area.'

'No.' She wanted to tell him all. 'But I will do soon.'

'You're moving here?'

'Yes — well, at least for the time being. I — I've just inherited a school at Millweir, that's a village a few miles from here.'

'Yes, I know it.' He stared at her across the small round table, not rudely, more in surprise, she thought. 'A school? You're a teacher?'

'No, I'm a nurse, but I can teach drama, as a therapist.'

He looked very alert, very interested. 'You specialise in difficult children, helping them, I mean?'

'No, I'm a registered nurse, but I've had some drama training. I hoped perhaps to combine the two, nursing and drama therapy,' she said in a burst of confidence. 'There was a hospital that was interested. . .' Her voice trailed off.

'It sounds eminently practical, combining two disciplines. Are you going to put this into action at the school you've inherited? Take difficult children or those with learning difficulties?'

'Perhaps. I don't know — I don't know if it's appropriate. I think the school is just a normal private school, it doesn't specialise. I — I don't really know very much about it. I've only just learned, you see, that I've. . .' Lucy shook her head and then lowered it over the table. She felt silly letting herself ramble on, she really shouldn't.

'That you've inherited the school?'

'Yes.'

'No wonder you were in a state of shock.' He hesitated for a moment with another forkful of teacake halfway to his mouth. 'Whoever left you the property, was he—she a relative?'

'No.' Again she had this overwhelming desire to tell this stranger more about her windfall. She leant slightly across the table, quite unconscious of how lovely she looked, with her cheeks delicately flushed from warmth and the stimulating effects of a thousand calories or so, and her hazel eyes sparkling greenly. 'I didn't even know them very well, the elderly couple who left me virtually everything, but they knew my parents.'

'And your parents?' His voice remained cool, impersonal.

'They died, a few months ago, they were both very ill.' She looked up at the man across the table through long curved lashes, and gave him a bleak smile. 'I daresay you think me very fanciful,' she said, 'but I don't think my father died of a myocardial infarct as the death certificate said, but of a broken heart.'

'No, I don't think that at all.' He sounded, for the first time, soft, gentle, though his eyes still remained stony, unyielding. 'We understand so little, don't we, about life and death and all that pertains to it?'

It was remarkable, Lucy thought, how softly a man with such a deep rumbly voice could speak.

She was about to answer when an insistent bleep-bleep-bleep interrupted.

'Oh, lord,' said her companion, consulting his watch and switching off the time bleep. 'I must go—duty calls.' He stood up and offered her a hand. 'Goodbye. Be guided by Clive...' She looked puzzled. 'de Winter,' he said.

'Oh, do you know him?'

'We were at school together. Great guy!' He squeezed her hand gently. 'By the way, how's the wrist?'

'Wrist?'

'You used your left hand to steady yourself when you stumbled in the office; I thought you might have sprained your wrist.'

She said in a surprised voice, 'I don't think so.' She stared down at her slender wrist and was surprised to see that it was faintly bruised, slightly swollen, and, now she thought about it, a little sore.

'Ah, I thought it might be,' said her table companion, bending over to inspect it. 'Get some hamamelis — witch hazel — from the chemist. It's great for bringing out bruises. Can you move your fingers?'

Lucy, mesmerised, moved her fingers as in a piano exercise.

'Splendid, don't let it get stiff.' It was an order, not a comforting comment.

'I won't.'

'Goodbye,' he nodded briskly.

'Goodbye.'

He left the tea-shop and she watched him stride away across the square and out of sight, huge black umbrella held aloft over his tall, broad-shouldered frame. Even from a distance he looked like a man who was quite sure of himself, no hang-ups, no doubts, a confident, sophisticated man, but cold, though he'd been kind to her in a fashion.

I wonder what his profession is? she thought as she gathered up her bits and pieces a few minutes later and prepared to return to the solicitor's office. A solicitor or lawyer perhaps, or a lecturer at the nearby university? Yes, he seemed to slot into that category; a philosopher maybe, which might account for his remark about life and death.

It had stopped raining and a shaft of late sunshine came out as she recrossed Market Square and made her way up the High Street to the offices of de Winter, Fraser, Formby and de Winter. Suddenly she felt as though a burden had been lifted from her shoulders. Life was good, she was happy. She didn't know what solution Clive de Winter might have come up with in the hour or so since she had left him, but she was certainly going to make the most of what was on offer.

'"Once more unto the breach",' she muttered softly as she mounted the white steps and let herself into the vestibule, her resolve and her hopes riding high.

CHAPTER TWO

Lucy spent the first few days following her meeting with Clive de Winter coming to terms with the extraordinary news that she was now heiress to an estate and a considerable fortune. The whole business was like a dream, a rags-to-riches story that churned endlessly round in her mind.

When she returned to the solicitors' office that first afternoon, after having tea in the Copper Kettle, she met Mr de Winter senior, an unworldly and old-fashioned gentleman who gave her sound advice about accepting her inheritance and enjoying it on a day-to-day basis. Lucy felt she could trust him utterly, just as she felt, with no valid reason, that she could trust the tall dark taciturn stranger with whom she had shared tea in the café in the Square. He too had suggested that she took up the challenge of taking on the school. Though why a complete stranger should trouble himself she couldn't imagine, especially someone who had seemed, though polite, remote, indifferent.

The de Winters, she discovered, had in her short absence arranged her affairs very satisfactorily. It had been agreed, by whatever authorities were involved, that she should take up residence in Mill School, prior to probate being granted. She would, in effect, be installed as proprietor of the school, Mr de Winter senior had explained, appointed interim administrator until such a time as all the legal matters had been cleared. It was within the powers of the executors to appoint such a person.

The relief of knowing that she no longer had a problem of where to live when she had to move out of her bedsit was tremendous. It was like a small miracle.

So too was the fact that she hadn't any financial reasons for continuing to work for the nursing agency, but years of training and a razor-sharp conscience wouldn't let her abandon the patient whom she was currently nursing.

In addition to wanting to keep faith with her patient, Lucy acknowledged the need to keep busy while waiting to move to Mill School. Work stopped her worrying too much about how she was going to cope with her elevated position and a staff loyal to the late Frobishers, who — and she had no illusions about this — might be hostile. Her inheritance, at least initially, was going to be a mixed blessing.

Tomorrow Clive de Winter was taking her to Mill School to meet the staff, a frightening hurdle, and one she would be glad to get over. Even now, in spite of having to stand in the dark and the pouring rain, waiting to fight her way on to the bus that would take her back to Islington and her bedsit, Lucy was glad she had decided to continue working. Nursing was her life, and, whatever was in store for her, she would always have her nursing training behind her. It was a reassuring thought.

She had been so busy with her thoughts that she was hardly aware that her bus was approaching, until the crowd around her started to surge forward, sweeping her along with them. With returning awareness came the realisation that all was not well, as out of the driving rain and the darkness splintered with light from shop windows and neon signs the bus came careering along, rocking and weaving from side to side.

It was going to crash. Lucy's heart leapt into her mouth. She seemed rooted to the spot. Someone screamed, there were other screams, shouts, the queue disintegrated, people pushed and pulled and stumbled against each other as the red double-decker monster came nearer and nearer. There was nowhere to go to get out of its path. The pavement was crowded. People pressed harder, wouldn't stop. Somebody slipped and fell on the wet ground. Lucy's brain began to function. She bent over the fallen figure and tried to help her stand up. Somebody else fell. The mass of people thrust themselves against her, and she was pushed into a shop doorway. The shrieks and shouts rose to a crescendo as the bus crashed into the bus-stop, ploughed into the people at the head of the queue, and slewed round till the rear smashed into the brilliantly lit window of a furniture shop. There was a sound of breaking glass, screeching brakes and the hissing of rain on hot metal, as the giant vehicle at last came to a halt.

Lucy, together with others nearby, was for a moment stunned into silence and immobility. She stood, as they did, frozen to the spot. All the normal sounds in the street seemed to have faded away, isolating the scene of the accident illuminated by the shop lights still blazing through the shattered glass. Everything had happened very fast, but now that the bus had stopped, shuddering violently as its powerful engine continued to throb, the scene took on a quality of still life to the watchers.

Then sounds from within and out of the accident area impinged again on her senses and spurred her into action. She pushed her way through the crowd milling around in all directions.

'I'm a nurse,' she said loudly, and was relieved to hear her own voice come out without a tremor in spite of her hammering heartbeats and inner fear. 'Somebody call for the police and an ambulance, and if there are any other medical people or first-aiders around come with me.' Cries and screams and moans were now coming from in and around the crashed vehicle.

She didn't wait to see what response her request had, but pushed forward till she came to the first casualty, a small child, whose legs looked as if they were pinned beneath the tilted-down tail platform of the bus where it was stuck through the jagged glass of the shop window. The child, a little boy, was screeching for his mother, and as Lucy crouched down to examine him, she could see a woman who looked as if she might be with the boy, half squashed by the rear tyres, a short distance away.

Lucy put her arms round the small victim. 'Listen, love,' she said softly, 'I'm going to look at your legs — I don't think they're hurt. Do you hurt anywhere else?' The child didn't answer, but continued to scream for his mother as Lucy looked closely at his legs and confirmed that they were uninjured, being several inches below the tailboard. Carefully she slid him out from beneath the vehicle. Miraculously he didn't even seem to be cut, though there was broken glass everywhere.

There was a woman crouching just behind her. 'Shall I take him, Nurse?' she asked, and stretched out willing arms.

'Please. I'm going to look at that lady.' Lucy indicated the ominously silent form partly concealed beneath the huge tyres of the bus. 'I think she may be his mum. She must be in pretty bad shape; the wheel's gone half over her chest and stomach. If you'll take care of the boy, I'll see if can do anything for her.'

The woman nodded and moved away carefully, making soothing noises to the frightened child.

Lucy eased herself forward trying to avoid the shards of glass that lay everywhere, glinting in the multi-coloured lights from shops and signs. The rain beat down relentlessly, stinging her face, blinding her eyes, as noise and movement went on around her.

The woman lay face upwards with the rain running

down her head, flattening her hair, making no impression on her wide open staring eyes. The rest of her body, what Lucy could see of it, was almost dry, sheltered by the bus and the huge tyres pressing against her chest and abdomen.

Lucy took the woman's temporal pulse, laying her fingers lightly at the side of the victim's head just above eyebrow level. Nothing, not a flutter. She crawled down beside the body and found a wrist and felt for a radial pulse. Nothing.

She could feel and hear somebody scrabbling over the pavement and odd bits of metal and glass behind her. A man appeared beside her.

'Anything?' he asked, clearly meaning a pulse or other signs of life.

'Nothing.'

'She must have massive internal injuries with that lot on her. And visible signs of injury that you can see? I can't get any further, I'm afraid, I'm too big.'

Before she could answer, out of the corner of her eye Lucy saw a flicker of light. 'Pupils fixed, unresponsive,' muttered the voice. 'Here, take this, and shine it down the length of the body and tell me what you see.' A small pencil torch was thrust into her hand from behind, and Lucy, recognising the voice of medical authority, did as she was asked and shone it along the still form, pushing herself further under the bus to do so.

The voice was familiar, deep, gravelly, but for the moment she couldn't place it. She looked over her shoulder as sharply as she dared. The bus was beginning to sway; she could hear it rather than see it. The floor of the bus seemed to be moving above her. It couldn't be. It was. She tilted her head. Very, very slowly it was keeling over. The great double-decker mass of the vehicle was moving down upon her.

'No!' she heard herself cry out, and then she was

clasped in a pair of strong arms and dragged backward away from the falling vehicle.

She wasn't sure how long the stranger held her, how long it took for him to drag her to safety, but suddenly there were other hands pulling at her, other voices reassuring her, hands restraining her. She struggled to free herself.

'Must go and help,' she insisted.

'You've done enough,' someone said. 'The ambulance people are here now. Let them get on with it.'

'No!' Her voice came out strongly. 'I'm a nurse, I must help if I can—there must be so many hurt. I'm fine now, I was just a bit shaken.'

'Are you sure?' somebody asked dubiously.

'Quite sure.'

'Well, your doctor friend's over there. He looks as if he can do with some help. I think he was almost as shocked as you were when he pulled you out from under.'

It was then that she recognised the man who was bending down over a huddled form lying in front of the shattered shop window as the stranger with whom she had had tea in the Copper Kettle a few days earlier. She'd wondered about his profession, and now she knew. Odd that she hadn't guessed. No wonder the voice of the man who had handed her the torch minutes before had sounded familiar. In the peculiar way that the mind functioned in crisis, all these thoughts rushed through her mind as she made her way towards him.

'How can I help?' she asked, reaching his side after scrabbling over bits of masonry dislodged by the bus as it swayed into the brick surround of the shop window. It remained there supported drunkenly against the wall. At least it looked for the moment relatively safe.

'Are you sure you're all right?' he countered, frowning. 'I don't want you passing out on me. You must have had a hell of a fright.'

'I'm a nurse, *Doctor*,' Lucy said with heavy sarcasm. 'I don't faint at the sight of blood.'

'Don't be silly, woman, that's obvious, but you were in shock a few moments ago. I need to be sure that you've quite recovered before you start assisting.'

Lucy swallowed her anger and nodded. He seemed to accept her confirmation. 'The paramedic has asked me to assess the injured outside the bus, until more ambulances arrive,' he told her. 'He and his team have gone on board the bus to check things out there. I don't envy them, poor devils. It must be pretty grim inside. Half the windows are smashed, and as for the driver. . .' He shrugged his broad shoulders. He looked sad and tired, and grimy with wet dust streaking his face and hair. Lucy had time to think that she must look a fright too. 'You go and check those two chaps over there while I finish looking at this lady. Let me know if you think they can be moved. The sooner we clear them away from the immediate area the better.'

'Will do.' She didn't feel angry any more, just grateful to be working with someone who knew what he was doing, though she realised that as he had taken instructions from the paramedic he wasn't a casualty officer. Presumably he, like her, just happened to be on the spot at the right time.

She scrambled over to where the two men lay side by side. One of them spoke as she got close. He had a cut that was bleeding profusely down one cheek, and he was making little moaning sounds of pain, but he stopped when Lucy crouched down beside him. 'My dad?' he asked. 'Is my dad all right' He turned his head to where the other man was lying.

'I'm just going to look. How about you?'

'I'm OK. Just tell me how my dad is — he's got a heart condition, so even if he's not hurt. . .' He tried to raise himself up on one shoulder, then collapsed back with an agonised cry.

'Stay put,' said Lucy firmly. 'You've got a broken arm or something. I'll go and look at your dad.'

She walked gingerly over the intervening space. Glass was the main hazard, great spikes of it glittering in the rain and artificial light.

Someone, it turned out to be the doctor, joined her as she reached the elderly man. They both bent over the still figure.

'His son.' Lucy indicated the younger man a short distance away. 'Says he has a heart condition.'

The doctor shone his pencil torch on the old man's face. There was a bluish ring round the mouth. 'And he's right,' he said tersely. 'I think his heart's had enough.' He examined the man's pupils, felt for a pulse, and listened over the chest wall for signs of life. 'Nothing,' he said. 'He's dead, I'm afraid.'

'Shouldn't we try to. . .?' The look on the doctor's face was enough.

'The poor old man's dead. We can't do anything more for him—let's see what we can do for the son.'

Lucy knew that he was right, that his decision was sensible, but part of her wanted to go on fighting for the old man's life. Surely there was something else they could do? If only there was a crash team around; they sometimes worked miracles. She looked beseechingly at the doctor.

'No,' he said harshly. 'We've got to help the others—come on.'

They returned to the younger man and the doctor confirmed what Lucy had suspected, that he had a fractured humerus and a fractured collarbone. While she and the doctor made his arm immobile, swabbed away the worst of the blood from his cheek and applied a dressing, Lucy tried to avoid giving the patient any direct information to him about his father. It was the doctor who eventually told him that his father was dead.

'A heart attack,' he explained. 'Probably before the bus actually collided with the bus stop. It must have been very quick—he wouldn't have suffered.' He patted the young man's good shoulder gently. 'I doubt if he knew anything about it,' he said.

How long after that she continued looking at the injured, binding cuts and giving painkilling injections supplied by the doctor from his case, she couldn't remember. At some point strong arms steered her into an ambulance and she was taken to the nearest hospital, where her various grazes and cuts, which she didn't remember collecting, were treated. An ambulance then took her home to Islington, where her usually indifferent landlady became embarrassingly kind and considerate, and made her a hot drink and ran a bath for her to have before going to bed.

The whole episode was like a dream-cum-nightmare. The following morning Lucy woke just in time to shower and dress before she took the train to Chelchester to meet Clive de Winter, who was taking her to Mill School to meet some of the staff. She found as she towelled herself dry that she had bruises in the most unlikely places, and that her hands were badly cut about, though she couldn't really account for them. Certainly she hadn't noticed while she and the doctor had worked to treat the injured.

The doctor—that was all she knew him as. It was an advance on the tall, dark stranger, which was how she had thought of him since the meeting in the Copper Kettle, but still hardly a complete picture. She must find out more about him from Clive de Winter, with whom he had been at school.

By eleven o'clock Lucy and Clive were at Mill School, and Lucy was being introduced to Miss Tarrant, the headmistress, a thin, frosty lady who barely succeeded in hiding her resentment of her new young employer.

'I hear from Mr de Winter,' she said, as though reluctant to believe him, 'that you're a *drama teacher* as well as a nurse.'

Lucy swallowed her irritation and smiled at the older woman. 'Well, not exactly, since I haven't had any practical experience in that field, but I have a degree in Related Arts which allows me to teach drama if I wish. I had hoped to combine it with nursing in teaching drama as a therapy at a very go-ahead hospital that was interested in the two disciplines. Unfortunately, economics reared its ugly head and that particular job didn't come about.'

Miss Tarrant's hostility was obvious. 'And are you planning to join the teaching staff here at Mill School, Miss Shaw, using drama as a therapy? I should tell you we already have a special needs teacher for the few children who have learning problems. It would be difficult to see where your particular skills would be useful.'

Lucy took another deep breath and kept her temper with difficulty. The woman was barely being polite, but according to Clive and Mr de Winter senior she was a wonderful teacher and a splendid headmistress, and Mill School and the Frobishers had been her life for a quarter of a century. I must make allowances, Lucy told herself.

'Perhaps, Miss Tarrant,' she said gently, 'you may be able to help me find a niche. Many of the best schools are now introducing drama as part of their regular curriculum, valuing it as an aid to English and literature, as well as character-building and self-confidence. I'm sure Mill School wouldn't want to be behind in such thinking.'

The head teacher flushed a dull shade of red. 'This school has always been in the forefront of educational advances, Miss Shaw, but we are not interested in some of the modern, gimmicky thinking that is swamping the system at the moment.'

'Well, I'm sure that with you here to guide me, Miss Tarrant, there'll be no danger of that.'

It was soon after this little exchange that Clive and Lucy left to return to the solicitor's office in Chelchester. Lucy's head was in a whirl. She had met so many people that morning — various teachers, including the secretary, Isabel Mottram, with whom she would work closely. Mrs Mottram, whom Clive had thought very friendly and willing to welcome Lucy warmly, was, Lucy thought, more dangerous than the openly hostile headmistress. She pretended friendship, and yet hated Lucy's advent at Mill School as passionately as Miss Tarrant.

The person whom Lucy most wanted to meet, because she felt they would be on the same wavelength, was the senior matron, sister in charge of the modern, well-equipped sanatorium, Ruth Lambert. However, when Lucy did a quick tour round that department, she learned from an assistant nurse that the matron was away at a relative's funeral.

'Please tell Matron that I'm looking forward to meeting her, Nurse. And thank you for showing me round.'

'Oh, I will, Miss Shaw. I know she was disappointed that she couldn't be here to meet you.' The young, pretty woman smiled cheerfully. 'It'll be lovely having a nurse at the helm, as it were. All the san staff are very pleased, so on behalf of us all, welcome aboard.'

The genuine warmth of the young nurse's welcome was a comfort to Lucy after her lukewarm reception by some of the other staff. She concentrated on this as they drove back to Chelchester. It looked as if the nursing contingent and perhaps most of the house matrons who were also attached to the sanatorium were going to be friends as well as employees, and if the sister in charge was as kind as she'd sounded there might be an occasional chance for Lucy to nurse in the school san.

At Clive's office there were yet more papers to sign, and it was as she finished doing this that she remembered to ask him about Doctor Stranger, the title she'd given the man with whom she had shared tea and the unpleasant task of assisting at the scene of the accident.

'Clive, I met a man coming into your office when I was leaving the other day — tall, dark, going grey. He's a doctor, he knew you at school. What's his name?'

For a moment Clive looked puzzled, then his face cleared. 'Oh, you must mean Hugh —— ' The telephone shrilled at his desk. 'Excuse me.' He smiled at Lucy as he picked up the receiver. 'Oh, lord! Yes, I was, sorry about that. I'll be there at once.' He replaced the receiver. 'Sorry, Lucy, I must rush off. I'm only half an hour late for an appointment.' He pulled a wry face. 'We stayed a bit too long at the school, I'm afraid, but I hope it was worth it. We'll do it again if we can before you take over. It'll be easier next time now you've broken the ice.'

'You've been very kind, Clive — many thanks.'

'Can I give you a lift anywhere?'

'No, thanks, I'm going to do a little sightseeing in Chelchester before I go back, get to know my future stamping ground, as it were.'

'Jolly good. You won't forget Friday night, will you? Dinner with us — Angela's dying to meet you.'

'I won't forget. Goodbye.'

Lucy left the offices of de Winter, Fraser, Formby and de Winter, went down the High Street and crossed Market Square and into the Copper Kettle. 'I just hope their lunches are as good as their teas,' she said to herself as she sat down at a window table and picked up the menu.

CHAPTER THREE

THREE weeks later Lucy moved into the Gatehouse, the private home at the end of the long drive leading to the school, where the Frobishers had lived for many years surrounded by their devoted staff and loving neighbours.

The Frobishers had a whole host of friends, thought Lucy. They were obviously very special people. 'Oh, please,' she prayed quietly to herself as the waiting weeks passed, 'let me live up to their standards. I just mustn't let them down.'

There was one person at least who didn't resent her inheritance — Angela de Winter. She and Lucy got on famously from the word go.

'I wish Jeanette and André had known you better,' Angela said within a few minutes of meeting her. 'They wanted to, you know, especially after your parents died. To them, you were almost like the daughter they never had. They told me as much after Jeanette had been in hospital and you nursed her.'

'Yes, I was sorry then that I hadn't known more of them, but they and my parents seemed to be implacable enemies for many years. Given a little more time, I believe I would have got closer to them, visited more often, but it was evidently not to be. I'm just going to make the best job of running the school that I possibly can, as a sort of memorial to them.'

'Well, you can count on me for all the help you may need,' said Angela. 'And try not to be too put off by some of the staff at the school. Believe me, they've all been well provided for by the Frobishers and have nothing to complain about.'

Following on that evening Lucy and Angela saw much of each other, and it was Angela who transported Lucy and her belongings that afternoon from London to Millweir and the Gatehouse.

But in spite of the rapport that existed between them, Lucy was pleased when Angela left to drive the few miles to the outskirts of Chelchester, where she and Clive and their family lived.

It was a relief to be on her own at last after the upheaval and almost perpetual tracking back and forth between London and Chelchester over the last few weeks. Now she could breathe again, and what was more, breathe the clean air of the countryside. Like the countryside in which she had grown up.

Resolutely she put aside memories of a happy and secure childhood and loving parents. Time enough to indulge in those sort of thoughts when she had settled into the cottage. At least now, thanks to the generosity of the Frobishers, she had security and the chance to build a satisfactory future.

There were occasions over the following days when Lucy nearly gave up. Miss Tarrant and Mrs Mottram, both indispensable to her and to the running of the school, continued to make life difficult each in her own way, refusing to respond to her genuine offer of friendship.

Only the sanatorium and the friendly reception she always had there from Matron Ruth Lambert and her staff offered warmth and sanctuary. It was a balm to her feeling of alienation to be invited to give the occasional injection, or treat a cut or sprained limb, or to be consulted about the condition of a young patient. As with Angela, Lucy had quickly formed a friendship with Ruth, with the additional bonus of having people and places in common, the world of medicine and nursing being a small one.

As she had known from the beginning, it was Mrs Mottram who was the most dangerous, because she was the more devious. It was she who, late one afternoon at the end of Lucy's second week at Mill School, announced that she was going on holiday the following week.

'But surely school staff have their holidays during school holidays? said Lucy in surprise, adding snappishly, for once not bothering to conceal her anger, 'You might have given me some warning!'

'Oh, this was specially arranged ages ago. My brother's coming home from India. I didn't think it would inconvenience you, Miss Shaw. Mr and Mrs Frobisher had agreed.' At the mention of their name, Mrs Mottram's eyes filled with tears. There was absolutely no doubt about the genuineness of her feelings for her late employers.

Lucy rushed to sympathise, her irritation with the woman swamped by a wish to comfort her. 'Oh, Mrs Mottram, please don't worry. I'll manage somehow. I dare say with all that's happened you simply forgot to mention it to me.'

Mrs Mottram contrived to look relieved, cunning and embarrassed all at the same time, knowing that Lucy was well aware that she had deliberately withheld the information about her holiday to be awkward, and yet was being disconcertingly nice about it.

'Well, I'll be off, then,' she said, putting the cover on her typewriter. 'See you in a fortnight's time.' She collected her coat and bag and put her hand on the doorknob, then turned back with what Lucy could only see as a sly expression. 'Oh, by the way, there's a Dr Bellamy coming to see you at six. He's hoping we can take his children at half-term. Oh, dear, I should have told you, shouldn't I? It just slipped my mind.'

Lucy turned her back on her secretary and pretended to look out through the rain-spattered window. She was damned if she would let the woman see that she was near to tears.

Of course it did,' she said, her voice rock-steady. 'Like your holiday plans. But then you've a lot on your mind at the moment, haven't you? Not to worry, I'll deal with it. We've certainly got a few spaces to fill.' She turned and smiled. 'Do enjoy yourself, Mrs Mottram. Goodbye.'

For the first time since Lucy Shaw had taken over Mill School, Isabel Mottram wondered if the young woman was quite as marshmallow-soft as she and Carol Tarrant had thought. Would their cold-war tactics freeze her out? There seemed to be a definite steely quality beneath that gentle and beautiful exterior.

Lucy stood in the window of her office looking out over the wide sweep of wet golden gravel that brought the drive to the elegant porticoed front door. She consulted her watch. It was twenty to six.

Squashing down all the bitter thoughts about Mrs Mottram, she concentrated on how to conduct the forthcoming interview. She had nothing to guide her. Miss Tarrant had handled the only other interview concerned with a child being admitted to the school a few days after Lucy's arrival. Lucy had appeared at the last minute and been reluctantly introduced by the head teacher as the new owner.

She sat down at her desk, pulled a blank piece of paper towards her and wrote: 'Name, address, children's names, ages, abilities or any special educational difficulties' — she didn't know if this was normal procedure, but decided that from now on it would be included in the questionnaire.

The front doorbell pealed out. She heard someone go to answer it. She took a few deep breaths, picked up her pen again and waited for the expected tap at her door.

It came a moment later. 'Come,' she called out authoritatively.

The door opened and June Powell, a junior housemistress, showed a flushed face round the door. 'There's a Dr Bellamy to see you, Miss Shaw. He says he has an appointment.'

'Yes, I am expecting him.'

'Oh, good, shall I show him in?'

'Please.'

Miss Powell disappeared back into the large front hall. Lucy heard a murmur of voices and then her door was pushed wide open and in came. . .the stranger. . . the doctor. . . Hugh. . .

She wouldn't let herself be surprised. Too many people had recently tried to deceive her. No way was she going to be outwitted or outsmarted by anyone again, not staff or so-called friends or seemingly impersonal strangers ready to take advantage of her openness and need to talk.

'Good afternoon, Dr Bellamy.' She held out a cool, nicely manicured hand. 'Do take a seat.' She indicated a chair placed at the ready opposite her.

'Good afternoon.' His voice was as deep and as drawling as she remembered. He smiled, a tight, controlled smile that didn't warm his eyes. 'So you decided to give this a go,' he said, waving an eloquent hand round the room to illustrate what he meant.

'Well, it was inevitable really. Rather a shock when I was first presented with the idea, but everything made sense later.' For some reason she was reluctant that he should have the satisfaction of knowing of his contribution to her determination to 'give it a go', a phrase, she thought, that didn't fit readily into this elegant man's vocabulary. It was as if he was making an effort to be friendly. 'Mr de Winter senior was very kind.

After he'd explained everything to me I knew I must make a stab at taking the school on.'

'I'm sure.'

'Now, Dr Bellamy, what can I do for you?' She was professional and detached. 'I understand from the diary that you're interested in placing your children here at Mill School, after half-term.'

His coolness matched hers. 'Yes. I have three children, twins, a boy and a girl, and an older girl. I understand they can be accommodated.'

'As day pupils?'

'Oh, yes, although there may be the odd occasion when I would want them to board. My job takes me away from time to time.'

'But surely you have someone to look after them? Your wife?'

For the first time he seemed somewhat disconcerted. 'My wife—I'm divorced. She...the children...of course I have a very good housekeeper, but she has her own life to lead and her times off sometimes clash with my duties. I'm hoping to improve these arrangements, but these things take time.'

His steel-grey eyes met hers very directly, revealing nothing, but Lucy had the uncanny feeling that he was flinching inwardly. Too much imagination, her father would have said.

She said hastily, not wanting to embarrass him, 'Your domestic arrangements are not important—or rather they are, but only in so far as they affect the children.'

Her visitor stood up, and for a moment she thought he was going to leave, too impatient to continue with the interview, but he took a few steps towards the window and then back again. She wouldn't have blamed him if he had turned and walked out—after all, he must have assumed that the wretched Mrs

Mottram would have passed on the basic information about his arrangements.

He put his hands on her desk and leant over it to speak to her. He looked what he was, a strong man speaking under duress. A man not used to revealing his feelings, but aware that on this occasion he must.

'It's because of difficulties with arranging care for the children, the right sort of care, that I hope to persuade you to take them occasionally as boarders should the need arise. Will you do that, Miss Shaw?' How he hated revealing his personal problems.

His square-jawed, lean, handsome face was only a few inches from her own.

She mustn't just give in because he was as near to pleading with her as a man of his type could be. 'I've first to confirm that I'll take them as pupils in any category,' she said, pursuing the impersonal line. 'Though of course it will be up to Miss Tarrant, the headmistress, and other senior teachers to confirm matters from the academic point of view.'

'Yes, of course, I do see that.' He reseated himself, and though he half smiled at her, she could see that his patience was wearing thin. He was anxious to get this uncomfortable interview over and done with. He was obviously a man used to controlling a situation, and must hate being put on the receiving end of an interrogation. 'Forgive me, I'm rather jumping the gun, but I do have to make arrangements as soon as possible, as I explained to your secretary.'

'Ah, yes—well, Mrs Mottram had to go away rather suddenly. Perhaps you'd be kind enough to fill me in on the situation.' Lucy clenched her teeth, but tried not to let it show. Isabel Mottram had a hell of a lot of explaining to do.

Dr Bellamy was looking at her across the desk. His face now wore a wickedly sardonic expression, with his well marked eyebrows raised into two triangles. He could see through her as if she were glass; no way was she going to be able to deceive him. 'You didn't know anything about my wanting to see you, did you, or even possibly the fact that I had an appointment, until a short while ago?'

His voice was oceans deep, sarcasm barely held back. He was too perceptive by half. He knew the difficulties she was having with some of her staff, as surely as if she had spelled it out to him.

Lucy prevaricated. 'Mrs Mottram has a lot on her mind—problems,' she waved her hand vaguely, 'she wasn't able to fill me in completely.' With an enormous effort she pulled herself together and became again very proper, very professional. Instinct told her that if she let this strong, hard man get the better of her he would probably despise her, and she would certainly lose any respect that he might have felt for her for taking on the school. For some inexplicable reason it seemed important that she kept his good opinion. She said, quietly, firmly, 'Now please, Dr Bellamy, do tell me about your children and their needs and your requirements, and we'll see what we can do to facilitate matters.'

He gave her a smile which curled up the corners of his mouth and left a sardonic gleam in his eye, which told her he was still reading her like a book. She blushed at what should have been her private thoughts concerning his opinion of her and fiercely told herself that he really couldn't read her mind, it was all in her imagination. She returned his smile.

'Right,' he said in his deep voice, 'I'll repeat what I told Mrs Mottram.'

'Please,' said Lucy huskily, 'do, but may I first have the children's names and ages?' Giving this practical information would give him a breather, allow him to marshal his thoughts and tell her whatever else was relevant that he felt she had to know, and for she herself to get herself properly together.

'There's Tess, she's the eldest, twelve and a half,' he began.

'Tess?'

'Yes, that's her baptismal name not a diminutive of any sort.' The expression on his face softened. 'We were into Thomas Hardy at the time, my wife and I.'

'Ah,' said Lucy, wondering if he was still in love with the woman from whom he was divorced. 'The D'Urbervilles' Tess?'

'Yes.' He was abrupt, dismissive; it seemed that he immediately regretted lowering his shield. 'And Piers and Chloe, they're twins aged nine.'

'And the address?'

'Old Rectory House, the Green, Millweir.'

'But that's Dr Hubbard's address. He's the school medical officer and the local GP.'

'Not any more.' He looked surprised. 'Surely you were told of this?'

'Told?'

'That Dr Hubbard has semi-retired and I'm taking over from him, though he's continuing to look after the school and a few special patients for a while?'

'No, no one has seen fit to tell me this, not even your precious Clive de Winter.' All the bitterness and humiliation that she had been suppressing over the last weeks suddenly surfaced.

Dr Bellamy said firmly, 'I'm sure Clive would have done so, but automatically assumed that someone here would have filled you in on the situation. After all, it's virtually an internal matter, and Dr Hubbard will still be attending the children here most of the time.'

Lucy took a few deep breaths from her diaphragm, making herself calm down. 'Yes, of course he would have said something—or Angela anyway. She certainly wouldn't have let me walk into this blind; she's already helped me over a few hurdles.'

'Angela's a lovely woman,' he said. 'I envy Clive.'

He wasn't just being placatory, he meant it. It was the nicest and most spontaneous thing that Lucy had heard him say. 'Yes, he is to be envied. Now please explain about yourself and Dr Hubbard, and what your roles are in relation to the school.'

'He's built a bungalow in the grounds of the Old Rectory and will continue to watch over the children here most of the time, and as I've said, is going to continue practising on a part-time basis, depending on his health. My family and I have just moved into the main house. There's a surgery attached, old-fashioned these days but a boon for me. I can do at least part of my work at home, so to speak, and be around for the children.'

Lucy wondered about his children. She looked at the grey salted black hair springing from the strongly marked widow's peak, at the arctic-grey eyes beneath the well marked black eyebrows, and the thin-lipped mouth set in a firm line. Fancy coming home to this austere, unbending sort of man every day. How did they make contact with him, or he with them, for that matter? She could imagine that when he wasn't seeing patients, he would be working on some erudite medical papers that only he and a few like-minded professionals could understand. Well, for what it was worth, she would do her best by the Bellamy children, and try to make up to them for the loss of their mother and their cold father.

Dr Bellamy looked at the expression on Lucy's face, and misinterpreted it. 'I know, it seems almost out of this world, doesn't it, these days? A home-based medical practice. But I work in association with the group in the next village and have more than adequate cover for nights or days off. But there will still be occasions when cover is difficult either at home or in the surgery, or when I attend the County Hospital in connection with my rehabilitation work. It was these sort of occasions that I had in mind when I asked you if you would board the children if necessary.'

'All right, Doctor, I can appreciate the problems that you might encounter on a day-to-day basis, and I dare say occasional provision for the children to board can be arranged.' She smiled at him, feeling for the moment that she was really in charge of the interview, and that she had retained the doctor's regard, but her vibes told her he was holding back something. Greatly daring, she asked, 'Is there anything else I should know, to do with the children or their circumstances?'

She felt more of a nurse for the moment than the proprietor of a school. The situation reminded her of occasions when she had had to prise information from a patient. Her over-active imagination working overtime again. This situation wasn't like any other that she'd handled. This man would tell her only what he wanted to tell her and nothing more. Unless. . .! Unless he was different where his children were concerned! After all, he was caring for them, when usually it was the wife in divorce cases who had custody of the children, and he had sounded quite — well, tender, when mentioning Tess's name, a brief glimpse of perhaps a softer man beneath the stern exterior?

There was a long silence, as Hugh Bellamy stared at her across the desk with his brilliant grey eyes. At last he seemed to reach a decision. 'Yes,' he said, 'you're right, there is something else. How very astute of you.'

Lucy shook her head, denying this.

Hugh Bellamy allowed himself a broad smile in appreciation of her cleverness. What an attractive mouth he's got, thought Lucy before she could stop herself, when it's not set in a grim straight line it's not really thin at all. 'Your Mrs Mottram,' he said in deceptively dulcet tones, 'needed much less convincing as to the needs of my children.'

'Mrs Mottram,' said Lucy, through compressed lips, 'is, after all, the secretary, however vital to this establishment. She is not the owner or administrator and ultimately responsible — perhaps that made it easier for her to take whatever you said at face value.' It sounded rather grand, she thought, but true.

'Ah, then she probably didn't think it was important that Tess has a little speech difficulty, a slight lisp combined with a stutter. Unfortunately, the divorce and matters leading up to it rather aggravated it. But I really believe that with the right sort of help and understanding, my daughter could be almost freed of this impediment. And you, Miss Shaw, as both a nurse and a drama teacher, must be ideally equipped to deal wth this mixed medical personality problem, mustn't you?'

He sounded genuinely grateful for the possibility, not as if he were buttering her up. Not that this grim, unyielding man would butter anybody up, but Lucy did have the idea that because his children, in his own remote fasion, were greatly loved by him, he might unbend enough to pursue their cause.

She chose her words with care. 'As a nurse, Dr Bellamy, I encountered this problem. Usually it was with young children sometimes diagnosed as needing psychiatric help. But you're right about drama teaching being beneficial, this has definitely proved to be helpful in some cases, and I would be only too happy to help Tess in this way. I presume you've tried all the usual methods available in this field?'

'She was boarding until a short while ago at a special needs school. She was desperately unhappy, and I felt that their other academic standards were not terrifcally high and she was missing out on those. She's a very able musician and a considerable mathematician, but everything for her revolves round her inability to speak a sentence without stammering. The lisp I think she could live with — in fact, in a woman a lisp can be quite attractive.' He produced the wintry smile that Lucy was growing used to. 'But the stutter, that's inhibiting.'

'Obviously there isn't any anatomical or physiological reason for her stutter?'

'Miss Shaw, I'm a doctor. Do you honestly think I would have allowed something so obvious as a physical cause pass me by?'

It was the nurse in Lucy who responded to this remark. 'No, Dr Bellamy, I don't really think you would, but you'd be surprised how often professionals make mistakes when it comes to their own family. I've seen it more than once. It would have been wrong of me not to ask, both as a nurse and as proprietor of this establishment.'

For the briefest possible moment, his grey eyes warmed. 'I'd have been disappointed had you not pursued the matter,' he said. 'When will you be able to give me a firm answer as to whether you accept Tess?'

'I'll have to speak to Miss Tarrant, but Monday or Tuesday, I'd think. Now, what about Piers and Chloe? Have they any particular problems'

'Nothing to compare with Tess's, but they're both still troubled about being separated from their mother and need gentle handling. Nothing, I'm sure, that you and your staff can't take care of. And Piers is prone to asthma, but responds well to his inhaler, and is sensible about using it. As a nurse you'll appreciate that he too has been affected by the tense emotional factors arising out of the divorce. But, like Tess, I'm sure he'll improve given the right help and environment.' Dr Bellamy gave Lucy a smile that this time almost reached his eyes. 'Your help, this environment,' he said, and his gravelly voice was almost velvet.

There was a moment's silence, then he asked, 'What

do you think, Miss Shaw, about the chances of the Bellamy children joining your establishment? Will they be acceptable?'

It would have cost him much to ask such a favour, and she wanted to say yes at once and take the bleak look out of his eyes, but she knew she must be sensible. After all, it was Miss Tarrant and her staff who would be mainly responsible for their day-to-day studies. At most, as a nurse, she might handle an asthma attack if Piers got into difficulties, or as a teacher of drama give Tess confidence in herself, enough perhaps to overcome some of her speech difficulties. She must be cautious.

'As I said, Dr Bellamy, I'll put it to the headmistress and other senior staff. I'll do this on Monday. . .'

'And phone me after your meeting with the decision, please?'

Lucy smiled. 'Yes, I'll do that. Of course, we'll want to meet the children.'

'Naturally, whenever you say.'

They shook hands. He had long, narrow hands, she noted, but strong — she had noticed that when they were dealing with the injured in the bus accident. She wondered whether to mention it, or if he would comment on the incident.

He kept her hand in his for a moment longer than necessary, then squeezed it gently. 'I see all your war wounds have healed,' he said, and his voice was a gentle as his handshake and his eyes gleamed silver and not arctic-grey. 'You were splendid that evening; a lot of people have reason to be grateful to you for your help.'

'No more than they should be to you.'

He shrugged his broad shoulders. 'It is, after all, my job.'

'And mine.' They smiled at each other, for the moment in complete accord.

'Well, goodbye,' He dropped her hand.

'Goodbye.' Lucy stood at the front door beneath the columned portico and watched him drive away into the darkness.

It had been a strange experience talking to him, he in the reluctant role of supplicant, she as potential provider for his needs. How he must have hated having to almost beg to have his children admitted here. What a rotten time they must have had over the last few years leading up to the divorce. She had some sympathy with his ex-wife; he must have been a very difficult man to live with, autocratic and serious. But why hadn't the ex Mrs Bellamy been given custody of the children? Because she didn't want them, or because she was considered unsuitable? And he must have appeared the most suitable parent to care for the children; that must surely be a mark in his favour.

The mind boggled, and Lucy reminded herself that she had problems of her own to solve without taking on the Bellamys. Just get old Tarrant to accept them as pupils and keep your mind on your work, she told herself as she closed the front door on the departing Dr Hugh Bellamy.

CHAPTER FOUR

IN THE event, Lucy didn't have to convince Miss Tarrant that accepting the Bellamy children as pupils might be a worthwhile challenge. Dr Hubbard, for whom Carol Tarrant had had a 'thing' for many years, had already spoken to her about his colleague's family, and she, to please him, was only too ready to support Lucy's suggestion that they should be considered for admission to Mill School.

She was less informed than Lucy about the children's various problems, because Dr Hubbard himself was not aware of the true situation. He knew only that the children were vaguely unhappy because of their parents' divorce.

Lucy, knowing she must be utterly honest about the matter, put Miss Tarrant and Basil Thorn, head of the boy's prep school and the English department, clearly in the picture.

'From what Dr Bellamy told me,' she said, facing the two senior teachers across her desk on Monday morning. 'Tess, in spite of her lisp and stammer, might present less of a problem than the younger children. Piers is an asthmatic and, I formed the impression, inclined to be awkward, and Chloe withdrawn since their parents' divorce. I think they might well be difficult.'

Miss Tarrant eyed her in a suspicious manner. 'Are you suggesting, Miss Shaw, that we,' she indicated Basil and herself, 'are not capable of handling *difficult* children? We are fairly experienced, you know.' She was being sarcastic and didn't try to hide it.

Lucy took in a deep breath to calm herself. 'I have

absolutely no doubts as to your ability or Basil's,' she smiled at him, and he beamed back at her, 'to handle any child, however difficult. You're the professionals, you know about these things. But I felt it only fair to fill you in on the background—Dr Bellamy was most insistent that we should know everything.' She resisted a temptation to cross her fingers as she gave her version of Dr Bellamy's interview.

'Of course, one would expect a colleague of dear Dr Hubbard to be explicit about his children's needs, however unpleasant.'

So Carol Tarrant is able to reconcile her conscience with her dear Dr Hubbard's request on behalf of the Bellamys. Love, even at a distance, makes fools of us all, thought Lucy.

Miss Tarrant might have an ulterior motive in wanting the children as pupils, but Basil Thorn certainly hadn't, yet he too said he would enjoy the challenge. He thought the special needs teacher would be able to cope with Tess and her stammer, and everyone would be helpful with Piers and Chloe—after all, the staff at Mill School had been chosen by the Frobishers because of their caring qualities as well as their academic ability.

'Perhaps,' said Miss Tarrant carefully, 'we should engage the special needs teacher on a full-time basis. There are other children who could do with more help. I think that's what the dear Frobishers would have decided.' Her faded blue eyes filled with tears, and for once she seemed quite natural with Lucy, neither icily polite nor dismissive.

'If you think it's a good idea, Miss Tarrant, I'll speak to the executors,' said Lucy. 'I'm sure they'll agree to our engaging this teacher full-time.'

Lucy saw no point in withholding the news from Dr Bellamy. She phoned his number just after eleven o'clock and got through immediately.

'Hello,' breathed a soft, sexy female voice in her ear. 'This is Dr Bellamy's residence. Can I help you?'

Expecting to hear either the doctor or the brisk voice of a receptionist, Lucy took a moment to recover from her surprise at the unexpected throbbing tones coming over the phone.

'Good morning,' she managed after a moment or two. 'May I speak to Dr Bellamy, please?'

'I'm so sorry, he's just left to go on his rounds. May I take a message?'

'Oh, no—well, yes, if you will.' She felt an absolute fool, not being able to make up her mind, but the voice had really thrown her. Could it be his housekeeper? 'Will you tell him that Lucy Shaw rang, please. He was expecting to hear from me. Ask him to contact me any time. Thank you.'

'He has your number?' asked the marvellous throaty voice amiably.

'Yes. I'm speaking from Mill School.'

The voice dropped another notch. 'Oh, the school, and you're *the* Miss Shaw. It is good news, isn't it? Poor lamb, Hugh's so terribly anxious to get the children sorted out.'

Surely it couldn't be the housekeeper. A friend? Hugh Bellamy a lamb? Lucy wanted to giggle. How much should I tell her? she thought. 'If you'll just ask him to call, please, many thanks.' She put the receiver down quickly, hoping she didn't seem rude.

About an hour later the phone rang in Lucy's office. This time it was the doctor himself. He sounded as calm as ever. 'Is it good news?' he asked. 'Hattie thought it might be.'

Hattie—obviously she of the sexy voice. 'Miss Tarrant and Mr Thorn have agreed that we should accept Tess and the twins,' she said. 'Would you like to come some time and look over the school and meet some of the staff and tie up the arrangements?'

'This afternoon, about five.?'

So soon? she thought, but kept her surprise to herself. 'Yes, I can manage that.'

'Splendid, I'll see you then. Goodbye.'

The receiver went down at his end before she'd hardly got her own goodbye out. His abruptness was irritating. He might at least have shown a bit more enthusiasm about the successful outcome of the matter, congratulated her perhaps on persuading her staff to accept his difficult brood. After all, it had been he who was so anxious to know the result of this morning's meeting, he who had almost begged her to intercede on his behalf.

Lucy tried to shake off her irritation and put the image of the handsome doctor out of her mind. He had been annoyingly present ever since her meeting with him on Friday. She hadn't been able to forget his piercing grey eyes, alternately gleaming with sardonic humour or bleak with restrained unhappiness.

Her thoughts had been dominated by him all the weekend. She had steeled herself to do battle on his behalf with the formidable Miss Tarrant, and yet he had just spoken as if the acceptance of his children at Mill School was a mere formality. Of course, he probably knew by now that his colleague Dr Hubbard had virtually achieved victory with the headmistress, and he was regretting lowering his defences in front of Lucy.

Well, if he wanted to be distant and professional and just another parent, she could match his impersonal attitude. When he came that evening, she would say a few words to him and then pass him over to the tender mercies of Carol Tarrant. Let him work his charm on that 'old trout', as Clive had once called her.

Dr Hugh Bellamy arrived nearly half an hour early for his appointment. Lucy was grubbing about in the minute front garden of the Gatehouse when his Range Rover pulled up on the drive. She had no idea who it was who had stopped since she was bent double beneath the hedge, trying to free a tiny cluster of winter cyclamens from the dead but strangulating tendrils of brambles.

'Oh, goodness!' she exclaimed as the wrought-iron gate squeaked open and the doctor appeared, towering over the hedge and the narrow flagged path. 'Surely it isn't five o'clock?'

'No, I'm early. I hoped to see you to apologise, before you handed me over to the formidable Miss Tarrant.'

What did this man have, second sight? How did he know that she was going to hand him over to the headmistress after the polite preliminaries? And apologise? What did he mean?

She stood up from her crouching position in one graceful movement and failed to see the appreciative look he gave her.

'Apologise?'

'For not thanking you properly for your efforts on behalf of myself and the children.'

She forgot her earlier anger. 'It was nothing,' she said. 'Your colleague Dr Hubbard had spoken to Miss Tarrant and she was convinced by him that accepting the Bellamy children would be a good thing.'

'And the other staff?'

'They're pleased to take on the challenge.'

'And that's your doing, Miss Shaw, for which I'm grateful.'

It would have been churlish to protest further.

'I won't be a minute,' she said. 'I must change my shoes and wash my hands.' She smiled and looked down at her mud-covered wellies and grubby hands. 'Do come in if you like, while I make myself presentable.'

'Thank you.' He ducked his head under the trellised porch and followed her into the tiny hall.

'Very nice,' he commented, studying the panelled walls and narrow staircase gleaming white against the thick nut-brown fitted carpet. 'Eighteenth-century?'

'Yes. I'm lucky, aren't I?' Lucy opened the door on the right. 'Please wait here in what's still quaintly named on the plans as the parlour. I'll not be long.'

'Yes,' murmured the doctor, inspecting the room with interest, 'you are lucky, Miss Shaw.'

The parlour, like the hall, was all gleaming white walls and nut-brown carpeting, with burnt orange curtains glowing at the latticed windows at either end of the long low room. Shelves full of books filled the recesses on either side of the elegant steel fireplace, where a wood fire blazed behind a brass fender. A round polished walnut table bore a sturdy vase full of early daffodils and drooping catkins shedding yellow-green pollen on the polished surface.

A chintz-covered sofa, two fat armchairs, a *chaise-longue* and several tall, rush-seated ladderbacks were dotted invitingly round the room. Matching the table standing beneath the front window stood an exquisite lady's escritoire, and at the other end of the room a glass bow-fronted cabinet full of tiny silver and china ornaments.

It was a delightful, lived-in, beautiful room which surely reflected the Frobishers' cultured and contented lifestyle. Lucy, thought Hugh, would live up to it, given a fair chance by the staff of Mill School.

Lucy, unaware of the doctor's thoughts, clumped through to the kitchen and into the small lobby at the back, divested herself of her boots and washed her hands at the kitchen sink. 'Would you like tea or coffee,' she called, 'before we go up to the school?'

'Neither, thanks.' He appeared in the kitchen doorway, filling it with his height and breadth. 'This is nice,' he remarked, looking with approval at the Aga and the more modern appliances fitted neatly round the walls; deep-freeze, fridge, microwave, dishwasher and washing-machine-cum-drier.

'Yes, the Frobishers, in spite of their prediliction for the old and antique, had all mod cons,' said Lucy.

'The better to do their job with, I imagine. Time for the children.'

Lucy nodded. She'd heard that compliment paid to the Frobishers *ad nauseam* since her arrival at Mill School. They were such paragons of virtue that she doubted whether she could ever emulate their achievements.

The doctor homed in with deadly accuracy on her thoughts. 'They must be a tough act to follow,' he said. 'But they obviously thought you capable, or they wouldn't have made you their heir.'

With so many people rooting for the late Frobishers she'd almost overlooked this fact. She smiled quite spontaneously. 'Yes, they must. Now if you'll excuse me for a moment, I've just got to comb my hair and make myself presentable,' she said, hoping he would stand aside and she could take herself upstairs to her bedroom.

'Why?' he asked, to his own surprise as well as Lucy's. 'You look perfect to me—beautifully windswept and with a smudge on your nose.'

Involuntarily she put a hand up to her nose. 'Where?'

'Here,' he said, tapping her nose gently. He took a large white handkerchief from his pocket, wetted it under the tap and proceeded to rub her nose clean. 'There now, even that slight but attractive blemish has gone.'

'Oh.' This intimate gesture, coming from this austere man, shook her considerably.

'Shall we walk up to the school,' he asked, 'or drive?'

Lucy cleared her throat. 'Let's walk. I can give you a guided tour as we do so.'

'Splendid.' They moved back through the tiny hall. Hugh opened the front door. 'Ready?'

She nodded.

They left the Gatehouse and started up the lane. The earlier rain had left the hedgerows glittering with prism-like drops of moisture.

'Spring,' said the doctor with restrained enthusiasm, 'as the poets constantly remind us, is magical.'

Lucy was surprised by his remark. 'Wonderful,' she agreed. She glanced across at the playing field nearby, where a game of hockey was in progress. 'Do any of your children play hockey, Dr Bellamy?'

He didn't have time to answer, for at that moment there was a shriek, and a cyclist careered round the bend in the drive ahead of them, clearly out of control. The front wheel of the bike hit one of the white marker stones lining the drive, stood up on end for a moment and then crashed to the ground. The woman rider was thrown several feet on to the grass verge.

Hugh Bellamy covered the few yards to the cyclist in a flash, while Lucy stood for a moment rooted to the spot, too surprised to move. Once she got over the shock, she too moved fast.

'What can I do?' she asked the doctor, who was kneeling beside the body of the woman and feeling for a temporal pulse. There was a trickle of blood oozing from a cut on her forehead.

'Fetch my bag from the car—here's the key.' He fished a bunch from his pocket. 'That one,' he said, singling out a black-headed key. As Lucy was about to speed off, he asked, 'Can you drive?'

'Yes.'

'Could you manage the Range Rover?'

'Of course.'

'Then drive back — we may need transport for this lady.'

'Right,' she called, already on her way down the drive. She noticed as she ran that the hockey players had seen the accident and a whole host of girls were tearing across the field to the fence.

She fumbled to open the unfamiliar car door and had the same problem fitting the key into the ignition, but once seated behind the wheel and taking a moment to familiarise herself with the gears and so on, she started the engine and moved up the drive.

As she rounded the first bend she saw that the doctor was still crouching beside the cyclist and the hockey players were lined up along the fence. She pulled to a halt beside Hugh Bellamy, who stood up as she came to a stop.

He gave her a reassuring smile. 'This lady's not too badly hurt, I think,' he said quietly. 'She's already come round from the slight concussion, but if you'll hand me my bag, I'll do a few tests before we move her.'

Lucy gave him the bag and climbed out. 'Can I do anything to help?' This was what she had asked him at the bus accident.

He shook his head. 'Not really, except reassure Mrs. . .' He smiled down at the plump, middle-aged lady.

Lucy smiled down at her too. 'It's Mrs Hurst, Doctor, one of our domestic ladies. How are you feeling, Ivy?'

'Not too bad, miss — a bit shaken, and my leg hurts.'

'Does your head hurt?' asked Hugh Bellamy, long fingers feeling gently over her scalp.

Ivy winced. 'That's a bit sore.'

'Yes, I'm not surprised, you've a nasty bump there, and a graze. Now I'm just going to shine this light into your eyes and I want you to look straight up at my forehead.'

Mrs Hurst did as she was instructed and moved her eyes in different directions when told to do so. The doctor looked closely at the cut on her forehead and her gashed leg.

'I think the best thing we can do is get you up to the school, Mrs Hurst, and with Matron's help I'll put a stitch or two in these cuts, and generally clean up your injuries. I should also like to take your blood-pressure and make sure you haven't got any internal damage. Will that be all right with you?'

'I won't have to go to hospital, will I?'

'I think it unlikely. Is there someone at home who could keep an eye on you tonight?'

'Oh, yes, my hubby and the lodger, they're both very good.'

'Fine.' He turned to Lucy. 'If you give me a hand, Miss Shaw, we'll get Mrs Hurst into the car. If you open up the back you can let the passenger seat down almost flat. I think Mrs Hurst will be more comfortable there.'

'Yes, of course, Doctor.' Lucy was glad to have something to do; so far she had felt totally useless. She moved round to open the back flap of the Range Rover, and received a barrage of questions from the hockey players.

'Is she badly hurt, Miss Shaw?' 'What made her come off?' and, 'Shall we tell Miss Tarrant or Matron?' and, 'How is she, has she broken anything? She went down with an awful bang!'

'Dr Bellamy thinks she's not badly hurt. We're taking her back up to the school. Somebody could warn Matron in sick bay and somebody else take a message to Miss Tarrant to explain that Dr Bellamy and I will be late for our meeting. Will somebody do that, please?' asked Lucy.

About half a dozen girls scrambled down from the fence. 'Two of you,' said Lucy firmly. 'And don't make a production out of it, just tell Matron and Miss Tarrant quietly what's happened.'

Penelope Fletcher, the head girl, detached herself from the group. She reminded Lucy of herself as head girl at her convent school some years earlier, serious, responsible but also full of fun and life.

'I'll go, Miss Shaw, and Lynnette will come with me,' said Penelope. 'The rest of you go back to the field and get everything packed up for the night, and explain to Miss Bull what's happened.'

Lucy looked at her watch. It was five-thirty. She called the head girl over. 'You take the message to Miss Tarrant, please, Penelope, and ask her if she'll be kind enough to wait till Dr Bellamy and I can join her, but if the other staff have to leave, we'll understand.'

'Will do, Miss Shaw. And what about Ivy's bike, shall I get someone to take it up to the school?'

'Please — how observant of you. I'd forgotten all about it.' They smiled at each other, and Lucy realised that she was nearer in age and certainly in temperament to the sixth-formers than to some of the senior staff. 'You get that organised.'

It was six o'clock before Dr Hugh Bellamy had finished dealing with Ivy and arranged with Matron for the patient's follow-up care. Lucy stayed for the first few minutes after they arrived at sick bay, but was happy to leave Hugh in Ruth Lambert's capable hands after she'd introduced them to each other.

She knew she was not needed in sick bay, and she was anxious to speak to Miss Tarrant and the other members of staff who might still be waiting to meet the doctor.

Basil wouldn't mind waiting; he lived in a staff cottage, as did Elizabeth Mayhew who taught maths, though she was a strange lady and not given to patience.

In fact all the staff waited to meet Hugh Bellamy. Lucy guessed this was mainly on account of his children and their special teaching needs, but also because he was their new GP and they were curious to meet him. The semi-retired Dr Hubbard was only going to be responsible for the children in future, and even that chore he would be sharing with his younger, very much fitter partner.

Lucy introduced the doctor, and over coffee and biscuits the staff and he got to know each other. He was of course bombarded with questions about the cycling incident, with everyone showing proper concern for Ivy Hurst. He was able to assure them that she had only minor injuries and that Matron was arranging to take her home shortly.

Miss Tarrant was anxious to know if the accident could have been attributed to the state of the drive and would Mrs Hurst be in a position to make a claim against the school.

Lucy, who hadn't considered such a possibility, wondered if the headmistress was being deliberately malicious and trying to stir up more problems, but there was nothing in her face to prove this. In fact she looked, as well as sounded, genuinely anxious when she put the question.

Hugh Bellamy said straight away, 'I don't think there's any question of that — Mrs Hurst was quite definite about the fall being her own fault. She was distracted by the hockey match, skidded on the wet surface and collided with a marker stone. Unless that could be considered a hazard for which the school is responsible. I'm sure there's no question of a claim. Though,' he turned and addressed Lucy directly, 'on reflection, it may be possible for you to claim for repairs to her bike on the school's insurance, which would perhaps be a nice gesture, coming from you to Mrs Hurst.'

His direct look and his words indicated that he was trying to give her a boost in front of her staff. Just as he'd guessed that her secretary had deliberately let her down, he now guessed she might be suspicious of the motive behind Miss Tarrant's question. He was offering her a chance to turn the situation to her advantage and play the magnanimous employer.

'What a good idea,' she said. 'I'll tackle them first thing tomorrow morning.' She smiled at the headmistress. 'What a good job you thought of claims and things, Miss Tarrant — it would never have occurred to me.'

With that parting shot she excused herself, saying she must go back to sick bay and check on the arrangements for Mrs Hurst's journey home. She turned to Hugh Bellamy. 'I must thank you, Doctor, for your help this evening. It was fortunate that you were on the spot to deal with this accident.' She smiled to take the edge off the stilted little speech, and hoped he would understand that she was also thanking him for his moral support.

'A baptism of fire in a small way, and with your nursing skill you would have managed admirably,' he said, matching her smile with a chilly one of his own. 'A small thing compared to the gratitude I feel for your help with my children. May I just ask before you leave me in Miss Tarrant's capable hands,' he inclined his handsome head toward the headmistress in a little bow, which she acknowledged with a pleased, gracious nod, 'if the drama lessons, for which I understand you're responsible, are part of the regular timetable or an optional extra?'

His question was so unexpected and so, at the moment, unanswerable as it hadn't even been discussed since her arrival at the school, that Lucy blushed and then paled while she thought of a suitable reply.

The doctor's question had fallen like a stone into the murmured conversation around them. There was a sudden and absolute silence, before everyone except Miss Tarrant became absorbed in loud discussions with their colleagues.

Hugh Bellamy's eyebrows arched dramatically. 'You are going to teach drama as a "therapy", Miss Shaw, are you not? It's one of the chief reasons for my wanting the children to come here to Mill School. I understood it was part of the curriculum, and I consider it an absolute necessity for the total well-being of my children. It's the sort of innovative thinking that most serious educators are recommending, I believe.'

His speech was so like the one that she had delivered to Miss Tarrant on the day that Clive de Winter had introduced her to the school that Lucy found herself looking towards the headmistress, testing her reaction, trying to establish if she remembered the occasion.

Surprisingly, Miss Tarrant smiled at her, a definite gleam of admiration in her eyes. It was she who replied to the doctor. 'You will appreciate, Dr Bellamy, that timetables for this term were already fixed before Miss Shaw's arrival. We haven't been able to discuss in detail when and how to include this interesting new tool of learning into the daily pattern. For the moment, I think we're all agreed,' her pale eyes swept over all those present, daring them to utter otherwise, 'that the subject will have to be an optional extra, but next term it will be part of our syllabus.'

Later, back in her cottage having satisfied herself about Mrs Hurst's condition, Lucy wondered about the doctor and the extraordinary way he had taken control of the evening. He had, to use her grandparent's phrase, 'charmed the birds off the tree', in spite of his remote and aloof air. No one, it seemed, was immune to his particular brand of steely reticence, warm approval and general charisma. Even Miss Tarrant had fallen victim to his courteous but firm handling of the evening's events.

I wonder, thought Lucy, as she turned on the wall lamps in the parlour and drew the curtains against the blustery dark of the evening, how much he believed of Carol Tarrant's hasty explanation about the drama lessons. All that rubbish about not having had time to discuss it! I'm sure he saw through it, but, tongue in cheek, was satisfied with the result for which he had laid the foundations in his clever fashion.

He's certainly a man to be reckoned with, and at the moment he seems to be on my side, thank God. I wonder how much our meeting in the Copper Kettle has influenced him. He certainly seems to think it's important that I can teach and nurse, and so do I. Perhaps I'll be able to match up to some of the Frobishers' perfections after all.

CHAPTER FIVE

LUCY woke the next morning with the feeling that something special and exciting was going to happen. Then she remembered—Hugh Bellamy was bringing his children to look round the school.

Hugh Bellamy! At the thought of seeing the doctor again so soon, her stomach churned over in an extraordinary manner, taking her completely by surprise. He certainly had a marvellous presence, and his dark good looks and piercing grey eyes were spectacular. Yet he was so remote, it was odd that he exuded such a strong, masculine charisma that he even succeeded in charming Miss Tarrant. No, charming was the wrong word, it was too superficial; what came over from the doctor was a strength and integrity. One felt he was utterly dependable in spite of, perhaps because of, his cool austere façade.

To be so affected by a man, and so quickly, was for Lucy a new experience. She, with her calm beauty, was more often on the giving rather than the receiving end of such emotions.

Sensibly she had long acknowledged that she was an attractive woman and that men usually succumbed to her fragile beauty like the proverbial bees to honey. With a couple of exceptions over the years, men had fallen for her rather than she for them. Often she had wished she might have a friendly relationship with a man, rather than a frenzied, often embarrassing and shortlived affair. Yet she was on the point of reversing the roles, of allowing herself to fall victim to the uncompromising Dr Hugh Bellamy. How ridiculous. She hardly knew the man, and what she did know made it clear that he was quite unaffected by her loveliness. His only interest in her was as the provider of care for his children. He had made that only too plain.

She must get a grip on herself, and exercise some self-control, but, try as she might, she couldn't squash the euphoria that enveloped her when she thought of the aloof, dignified doctor. Perhaps because other men so readily succumbed to her, some inner compulsion was driving her forward to win the interest of Dr Bellamy. No, she wasn't that sort of woman; she wouldn't play with anybody's emotions to satisfy her vanity.

It was a lovely spring morning, all blue and gold, with the sunlight glittering on wet leaves and early daffodils. Lucy opened her casement window wide and leaned out, breathing in the fresh morning air and trying to still her bumping heartbeats. It was ridiculous, absurd, she told herself, to be so affected by a man, any man, at her age, especially one whom she had met briefly over several weeks, at intervals. All right if you were eighteen, but at twenty-six? Ludicrous. Rationalising her feelings made no difference whatsoever. She grinned like an idiot at herself in the mirror and tralaahed a bar or two of an old song about a man being big and strong.

'Lucy Shaw, you are a fool,' she told her reflection, and smiled at how little it mattered. With a great sigh of relief she realised that whatever the cause, for the first time since the trauma of her parents' illness and death she felt free to be happy. It was a wonderful feeling. Wonderful, but something—well, at least his part in it—that she would have to suppress when she met the doctor again. No way must he guess at the overwhelming effect he was having on her; at the very least it would embarrass him, at the worst make him even more remote.

She had no wish to see him react like this in either direction. However much she was affected by the situation, she must not let him ruffle her cool.

Bearing this in mind, when Hugh arrived with his children mid-morning as arranged, Lucy gave him a pleasant but businesslike welcome.

The Bellamy children were all three good-looking, but Tess was quite beautiful, with a sleek cap of black hair and dazzling blue eyes. As if she was being compensated for her speech defect by being ravishingly lovely, thought Lucy, taking the girl's hand and wishing her welcome. She was surprised by the calm and confident though restrained manner with which Tess responded. Truly the daughter of the sophisticated father.

The younger children were wary and withdrawn, though perfectly polite. They shook hands solemnly and said, 'How do you do?' in muffled tones.

The started their tour in the main house, with the junior classrooms on the ground floor and the music, art, study rooms and library on the floor above.

They walked along the wide, elegant corridors of the one-time country house, the nucleus of the present-day bright modern school, the brainchild of the Frobishers. As always, when walking through the lovely old Georgian building, Lucy was overwhelmed by it all and conscious of her shortcomings. How was she ever going to manage such an undertaking?

Something of her thoughts must have shown in her face, for Hugh put a hand on her arm and asked if she was all right. He asked in the professional voice of a doctor, not concerned as a friend might be, and it served as further warning to her not to betray her feelings to this automaton of a man.

'Oh, I'm fine,' she said, moving smartly out of reach. 'It's just that I haven't yet got used to the idea of being responsible for all this.' She waved a slim hand around, indicating the elegant mouldings on the ceiling, the tall window at the end of the long corridor, and the wide grand staircase, balustraded in dark polished oak. She raised neat eyebrows over her green almond eyes which were twinkling with a wry humour. 'And that's before I even begin to worry about my ability to administer the school and the children.'

'Oh, I think you'll cope, Miss Shaw, an excellent nurse like you. You've the right sort of background and training for it.'

He obviously meant to be encouraging, but his remark was made in his usual unemotional tones, and Lucy decided to take it with a pinch of salt. He was just being polite, she decided.

On the first floor, Tess began to show some interest in her surroundings. The music-room clearly delighted her. It was empty at the moment, and she wandered round running her fingers over the keys of the grand piano and the two uprights, and stopped to pluck at the harp in passing. She also examined with interest the other instruments in the large room.

'This is brilliant,' she said, 'absolutely brilliant.' She turned her serene face towards Lucy and almost smiled.

Lucy sighed with relief. At least one of the Bellamy children seemed prepared to find something good about Mill School.

They had a quick tour of the dormitory floor and then started on the newer buildings, built out in two wings from each end of the main house. Two storeys high and built of mellow red, almost pink bricks, they had been designed to sit in with the plain Georgian architecture of the original building. These wings housed the senior pupils and the science and computer-rooms. A glassed-in corridor connected one of the wings to the sanatorium, and several other outbuildings, including a squash court and a pottery workshop.

Although he had seen and admired the excellent sanatorium on the night of Mrs Hurst's cycling accident, Hugh Bellamy found everything larger and more impressive than he'd imagined. No wonder, he thought, the attractive Miss Shaw is rather overwhelmed — she's inherited an awesome responsibility. He felt an unexpected and unwelcome rush of protectiveness towards this brown-haired young woman, as beautiful in her way as his Tess was in hers. And, he thought, with uncharacteristic ruefulness, not a lot older, by the look of her, though from what he had gleaned from conversations with the de Winters she must be well into her twenties. Not that it mattered to him; he had nothing but a professional interest in Lucy Shaw, or any other woman. Women were, and had been, off limits since his wife had deserted him. His life, now and in the future, revolved round his children and his work.

Both the younger children remained indifferent to all that they were shown, until they went outside and saw the opaque dome of the swimming-pool, when they became, for the first time, quite animated.

'The twins have ambitions to reach Olympic standard in swimming,' explained Hugh. 'Hence the enthusiasm.'

'Oh, that's splendid,' said Lucy, relieved that there was something that might break through their polite but restrained behaviour. 'The sports staff will be delighted.'

At the end of their tour, Lucy conducted the Bellamys to Miss Tarrant's study, and left them to be interrogated by that formidable lady. Would the headmistress respond so readily to the doctor's magnetism today, she wondered, or would the presence of his children alter her approach?

* * *

Well, whatever Miss Tarrant's reaction was, Lucy found to her annoyance that in spite of being very busy all afternoon she could not get the image of the doctor out of her head. She had seen another side of the man that morning, an affectionate and caring father in close rapport with his children. They seemed not to be in the least daunted by his remoteness, in fact that aspect of him dissolved in front of his offspring, and he became a loving and almost indulgent father.

It made Lucy wonder afresh how, in spite of his obvious faults, any woman could walk out on him and those stunning children. How could any mother leave them?

Of course, there was always the possibility that Dr Bellamy might be a splendid doctor and devoted father, but a less than devoted husband. . . No, surely not. He couldn't be a philanderer, not with his cold temperament. How do you know that? asked a jeering inner voice. You know nothing about the man. What about the sexy-voiced Hattie, she who had called Hugh 'poor lamb', where did she fit in to the Bellamy ménage? Was the haughty doctor having a scorching affair with her? A phrase much quoted by her mother came to mind. 'Still waters run deep', she had frequently opined.

Resolutely Lucy squashed all thoughts of the doctor and his family and concentrated on work.

Relegating the fascinating Dr Bellamy to the back of her mind became easier after a few days. She was extremely busy even over half-term, which was for Mill School simply an extended weekend, with many of, but not all, the boarders away. It was an ideal time for her to do a thorough inspection of all departments and socialise with the staff who were still on duty or who had remained on the school premises, for although it was now some weeks since she had moved into the Gatehouse, she didn't yet feel that she properly belonged to the community.

Miss Tarrant, since the evening with Hugh Bellamy and her open acceptance of the role that Lucy would play as a drama teacher, was rather less acid. She made a point of fully discussing with her, as a nurse as well as drama teacher, the extended role that the special needs teacher might play. The special teacher herself was only too willing to discuss her work, not only in relation to Tess Bellamy and her stutter, but other children with varying needs. She was pleased to have Lucy's support and willingly gave hers to the setting up of drama classes over which Lucy presided.

In fact, it surprised even Lucy how quickly some of the more reticent or backward children responded to acting out their problems, and several teachers remarked on the improvement in their work.

Halfway through the second half of the spring term, a mini-epidemic struck the school. Ruth Lambert, the matron, reported one morning that two boarders had woken feeling unwell, with raised temperatures and other flu-like symptoms, and one child had the beginnings of a rash.

'I'm almost certain it's rubella—German measles—and not measles or scarlet fever,' said Ruth. 'One child has slightly swollen glands, though the other hasn't yet produced these. I've informed Dr Hubbard, and either he or Dr Bellamy will be up shortly. I'd like you to be here when the MO comes so that we can discuss control measures if necessary and notification of parents.'

'It sounds rather alarming, Ruth, control measures and notifying parents—after all, rubella's not normally serious.'

As a nurse, she was surprised by Ruth's reaction to this generally accepted childhood disease, which rarely had any compliations.

Ruth said cheerfully. 'Of course it's not, as you well know, but if it is rubella we're probably in for a mini-epidemic, which certainly has a nuisance value at the very least in a school of this size, though the children only feel ill for a day or so.'

'And if it isn't rubella? Could it be something more serious?' Lucy's mind was doing somersaults trying to remember what she knew of childhood complaints and how they presented. Her recent nursing experience with the agency hadn't produced much in the way of children's nursing.

'Could be,' said Ruth, sounding quite calm and unflappable. 'Which is why I want a doctor up here immediately, to confirm the diagnosis. But not to worry, Lucy, everything will be OK.'

'It sounds most unlikely to me,' said Lucy gloomily, thinking of parents having to be notified and all manner of things to be done, because this was a school for which she was responsible, and not a hospital ward. 'I'll be over at once.'

In the short while that it took her to walk from the house to the sanatorium, discreetly placed in a grove of trees and isolated by a glass corridor from the main building, another child had reported sick. As Lucy entered the san, Dr Bellamy drew up to the outside door in his Range Rover. It was the first time she had seen him for days, and, anxious as she was about the children, she was quite shaken by the effect he had on her. But her reaction was at least tempered by relief that he had responded so quickly to Ruth's request for a medical opinion, and her anxiety for the children made it easy for her to squash her personal feelings.

'Morning,' he said casually as he stepped out of his car and turned to retrieve his surgical case. 'I understand we have a spot of bother.'

'You could say that.' Lucy frowned as she peered at him through the bright sunlight which was aggravating the headache that had started a short while before.

'Don't look so worried, my dear, children are prone

to all these infections, and generally speaking it's good to get them over with when they're young.' He smiled kindly at her and Lucy gritted her teeth — as if, as a nurse, she didn't know all that. The last thing she wanted at the moment was to be patronised; she wanted the truth.

This was her first big problem, she realised, something that as the owner or temporary administrator of Mill School she would have to deal with. This was her resonsibility, not Miss Tarrant's as headmistress, or Ruth Lambert's as matron, but hers, Lucy Shaw's. She would have to field anxious enquiries from parents, and she would, with perhaps the support of the governors, have to decide on quarantine, the curtailment of lessons, and other factors. Her mind boggled. This was an aspect of school administration that she hadn't considered, or been warned about. She wished she felt brighter, more alert, less headachey.

She squared her shoulders and put up her chin. 'Shall we go in and look at the invalids?' She sounded rather defiant.

Hugh Bellamy was unaffected by her attitude. 'That's what I'm here for,' he said calmly.

He stood aside for her to precede him through the door. Together they walked down the short corridor to sick bay. Ruth was waiting for them.

'I don't think there's much doubt,' she told the doctor, 'that it's rubella.'

'Let's have a look at them.'

Thank goodness for that, thought Lucy as she watched as the doctor examined the three children with Ruth's assistance. He ran his long fingers down their necks behind their ears, and nodded. 'Glands are coming up,' he said, smiling at each child in turn. 'You'll feel better by tomorrow or the next day. Now let's see what sort of temperatures you have.' Ruth popped a thermometer into each child's mouth while

Hugh listened to their small chests through his stethoscope. 'Fine,' he said. 'Nothing to worry about — all you lucky young ladies have German measles. Now, do you know why I say lucky?'

Two of them shook their heads, but the third, a ten-year-old, said, 'Because it's important for females to have German measles when they're young, or to have an injection to stop them getting it later when they have babies.'

'Well done, absolutely right. German measles is a very mild illness, rarely producing or having any side effects, but a pregnant woman may pass on some disability to her unborn infant. That's why you three are lucky, you won't have to have a preventative injection at a later date. You've immunised yourselves by catching the dreaded lurgi.' He made a face at them and the girls giggled. 'Right, I'll be off now, ladies. Goodbye. Do as Matron tells you and you'll all soon be up and about.'

He smiled and turned to wave to the girls as he, Lucy and Ruth left the dormitory to have a council of war in the sanatorium office. He really was a smashing doctor, Lucy thought, and how amazing that he should let his guard down to such an extent that he could joke with the children. Gone was the remote man who normally confronted the world.

Lucy felt quite weak with relief that the infection had been confirmed as rubella. She would still have plenty of work to do notifying parents, but at least it was unlikely that any child would be seriously ill, and she could make herself useful assisting with the nursing. She sat down heavily in a chair by the desk.

'Are you all right, Lucy?' asked the doctor sharply, bending over to peer into her face. He grinned engagingly. 'You haven't got the old rubella bug, have you?'

He'd called her Lucy! Had he meant to, had he noticed? Was it in the least bit important to him? She had been pale with relief, but now she felt her cheeks getting hot and red. It was absolutely ridiculous to be thrilled because a man had called her by her first name. The fact that most people did so within a short while of meeting had nothing to do with it; this austere man, with hard unsmiling eyes and mouth was not most people. Even seeing him as a loving father and a kind doctor hadn't made him seem less aloof or reticent with her.

Dr Bellamy was not a man to form quick friendships, not a man to be familiar, not a man to use first names casually, rashly.

'Lucy, have you had German measles?' He was standing in front of her now, his hands on her shoulders. His voice was firm, demanding an answer. Professional.

'I don't know — I don't remember.'

He asked patiently. 'Do you recall having a vaccination at school, the sort of thing I was talking to the children about, when you would have been between eleven and fourteen?'

'I'm sorry, I just don't remember,' she told him.

'Well, not to worry, your GP will have your notes. Who are you registered with?'

'Oh, I hadn't thought. Not with anybody yet. I haven't changed my doctor since I was at home with my parents.' Lucy suddenly realised where all this questioning was leading. 'Look,' she said, standing up, though her legs felt like cotton wool, 'there's nothing wrong with me, it's the children we have to worry about, and letting their parents know, and checking up on the others.' She faced Hugh Bellamy. 'Doctor, please do what you've been called in to do, confirm this diagnosis and instruct Matron and me as to the care of the sick children.'

She was so angry that she failed to be surprised by her words or attitude. She didn't care what Dr Bellamy thought. It was annoying that her headache persisted and she couldn't focus properly. Both Hugh and Ruth were looking hard at her, but their faces were strangely fuzzy. The doctor pushed gently on her shoulders and eased her back on to the chair. He placed a beautifully cool hand on her forehead, and said something to Ruth which sounded like 'temp sky-high'. His fingers were on her neck, and he was speaking again, but his words were slurred; she couldn't understand anything.

It was dusk, she realised, surfacing some hours later. Sister Sue Martin, the deputy, part-time matron, was in the room.

'Ah, awake at last,' she said.

'Awake?' Lucy pushed herself up in the bed and examined her surroundings. 'Of course, I'm in the san. I was awake earlier, wasn't I, but surely you weren't on duty then?' Her throat hurt when she spoke.

'No, I came on about an hour ago. You passed out in here this morning, don't you remember? You've got this beastly rubella thing, I'm afraid, and Dr Bellamy insisted that you be nursed here.'

'Oh, he did, did he?' Lucy felt irritated that he should have made such a decision on her behalf. What had it got to do with him? 'For heaven's sake, I'm quite capable of looking after myself in the Gatehouse for a few hours till I get over the worst of this. After all, it's only German measles.' She realised how cross she sounded and her voice seemed to be giving out. 'Sorry, Sue, I didn't mean to get at you. I'm just furious for myself for picking up this wretched infection, and passing out, of all things. I can't believe that a little thing like this made me faint.' She swallowed hard and tried to ignore her painful throat.

'Well, Dr Bellamy thinks you might be a bit run down, which made you an easy target for the bug, and of course all these childhood things are worse for adults. Now I won't be a minute, I've got to let Ruth know you're awake.'

Sue was back from the office in a short while. 'I'm going to take your temp and pulse now, and then you can have a drink.' She put a thermometer under Lucy's tongue. The sister's fingers felt very cool against her hot sweaty skin. She removed the thermometer after a minute. 'There, now you can have a drink.'

Lucy drank thirstily. 'Gosh, I needed that.'

'I'm not surprised—what with a high temp, sore throat and swollen glands. You can drink all you want, in fact the more the better, as you well know. If you do that you'll be a model patient, and the super Dr Bellamy will be very pleased with you.' Sue grinned, and Lucy returned her smile tremulously, feeling ridiculously weak and, of all things, tearful. The super Dr Bellamy indeed, she thought indignantly.

Ruth arrived at that moment, and Lucy wasted no time in taking out her frustration on her. 'Why on earth did you let that Dr Bellamy arrange for me to stay here?' she asked in what she meant to be a firm, demanding voice, but which in fact came out in a croaky whisper. 'I could easily look after myself.'

Ruth ignored the outburst. 'Yes, of course you could,' she said placatingly. 'But it seemed sensible to put you to bed here where we can keep an eye on you for a couple of days—and,' she added cunningly, 'where I can keep you informed about our little epidemic. You'd have been quite cut off from events if you were in bed at the Gatehouse.'

'Don't be so bloody reasonable, Ruth!' snapped Lucy, wanting to be fierce but failing miserably with her cracked voice. 'God, I sound pathetic, don't I?'

'Yes,' said Ruth and Sue together.

Suddenly Lucy's ill humour left her. She was lucky to have two friendly trained nurses to look after her, even if the masterful Dr Bellamy had organised it. She giggled, but even that hurt. 'Do whatever you want with me,' she rasped painfully. 'I'm all yours.'

'Right,' said Ruth, rolling up her sleeves. 'A tepid sponging to help bring that temperature down and some nice cool, clean bedclothes. How does that grab you?'

'Pure luxury,' murmured Lucy in her hoarse voice.

She was still feeling better-tempered and certainly more human in a pair of her own neat cotton pyjamas, when the doctor called in to see her, and, to her chagrin, sent her pulses racing.

'How's the invalid?' he asked in what she imagined was a patronising, avuncular tone that he might use with one of his children.

'Oh, much better, thank you,' she replied in what should have been a throwaway, gracious manner, had her vocal cords not let her down. She'd forgotten they were barely functioning, between a sore throat and swollen glands. She sounded like a Twenties singer on an old, cracked seventy-eight gramophone record.

Hugh Bellamy suppressed a grin which even reached his grey eyes and astonishingly made them twinkle, something Lucy would have thought impossible until she had seen him with his own children, and the girls in sick bay that morning. He sat down on the side of her bed. 'I'm glad to hear it,' he said. 'But you really will feel better in a couple of days.' He placed his fingers on her pulse, nodding as he released her wrist and compared his findings to the chart on the bedside table. 'Good, slightly improved, and your temperature's beginning to come down. But I want you to keep on with the medication and drink as much as you can. You're a bit run down. I think you might be anaemic. May I?' he leaned forward and pulled down her bottom eyelids. 'H'mm, yes, it looks like it, but I'd like to confirm it with a blood test. Have you any history of anaemia, do you know?'

Lucy shook her head. She didn't trust herself to speak with her squeaky voice, which would be made worse, she fancied, by her own reaction to his touch.

'Well, perhaps we can talk about it tomorrow when you have your voice back. Sleep well. I'll be in first thing in the morning to give you a report on the children, but rest assured, they're all being looked after by your devoted staff. Goodnight, Lucy.'

He was gone before she could utter even a squeak, having completely redeemed himself of his earlier patronising manner by recognising her authority where the children and her staff were concerned. Sue Martin was right, he was a stunning doctor, and she should be pleased that he was involved with the school and with herself.

If only he didn't make her feel so vulnerable whenever he was around, if only she could convince herself that he was a sophisticated intellectual with no interest in women, especially young, beautiful women. From all that she was beginning to hear, Hugh Bellamy was a disappointed man where the woman in his life was concerned. Rumour had it that he was still in love with his wife, that he was a one-woman guy, and unlikely to look elsewhere for solace. There was just one thing on which rumour was silent, though many made an attempt to fill the void, and that was the sexy Hattie. No one seemed clear about who she was, or what she was doing in the Old Rectory.

The situation was unnerving, but something she would have to learn to live with, Lucy decided as she slipped into oblivion.

CHAPTER SIX

As HUGH had predicted, Lucy was up and about within three days, and with iron-based medication to treat her mild anaemia, was soon on the mend.

She returned to the Gatehouse with pleasure and relief. More and more she was valuing her independence and the feeling of having her own home around her. She thought often about the Frobishers, whose shoes she was trying so hard to fill, and about her own parents who had at one time been their friends. More then ever she regretted the wasted years, and more than ever was glad that she had turned from acting to nursing, which had brought her again into contact with the Frobishers. She counted herself doubly fortunate to be able to indulge her old love of acting in a small way, by taking drama classes, which she found rewarding, while still practising nursing to a modest degree.

Deep in her heart she knew too that she was grateful for the change in fortune that had brought her to Mill School, and, because of that, into the orbit of Dr Hugh Bellamy.

It was no use pretending any more; she was strongly attracted to this man, though he was cool to the point of coldness, except when he had treated her as a patient. Then he had been kind and gentle. But I can't go on being an invalid just to make him be nice to me, Lucy admitted to herself with grim humour. She wondered if she was expecting too much from the doctor, and if it was only in her imagination that he seemed stiff and formal. All the other staff seemed to think that, though he was reserved and a perfectionist where work was concerned, he was quite friendly and approachable.

'He doesn't smile a lot,' said one of the nurses, 'but then from what I hear about his ex-wife, he hasn't a lot to smile about. She seems to have led him quite a dance, poor man.'

Lucy would have liked to have kept the conversation going, but felt it wouldn't be proper to do so. She had never been much interested in gossip, and in this case it seemed wrong to be speculating on her medical officer's domestic affairs. She recalled only too vividly how difficult he had found it to discuss them when he had come to see her about admitting the children to the school. He was a very private man, and no way would she invade his privacy.

'Well, we're lucky to have such a good doctor to look after the children,' she said to Nurse Brent, helping her to strip and remake a bed in sick bay. 'What a good thing he seems to be able to cope with us and with his village practice, since old Dr Hubbard is still poorly.'

Nurse Brent, suitably diverted, chatted on about Dr Hubbard, whom she'd known since she was a baby, until they finished their bedmaking and started on checking the medicines in stock.

The rubella epidemic had proved a blessing in disguise for Lucy, for it catapulted her into a strong position where nursing and the sanatorium was concerned. Once she was fit enough, she took over duties from Matron Ruth and some of the other nurses who were stretched, and won the respect of most of the staff who had hitherto tried to make life difficult for her.

When one of the assistant part-time sisters announced that she was pregnant and wanted to stop working, Lucy seized the opportunity to offer her services, and Ruth Lambert, with whom she had forged a strong friendship, was only too pleased to take her up on the suggestion that she would fill in the vacant hours.

'If you're sure you can manage? It'll be so much nicer having you,' she said, 'rather than breaking in a stranger. But you mustn't overdo it because you're feeling better, you've plenty to get on with running Mill School.'

'Well, there's a very competent and experienced board of teachers and governors to do that,' Lucy pointed out. 'And as for the volume of nursing—come off it, Ruth, you know that apart from the odd emergency, nursing here's a doddle compared to hospital work.'

'Agreed, although I don't know whether I should admit as much to my employer.' Ruth grinned and dodged the balled-up tissue that Lucy aimed at her. 'But you're taking quite a number of drama classes now, and when we get to next term, the summer term, I can tell you things really begin to hot up around here.'

'Yes, I seem to remember paying a good many visits to the san when I was at school, when cricket and tennis and all the other outdoor things got going. Tell me, what are the chief problems connected with the children in the summer term?'

It was mid-morning, and they were sitting in Ruth's office having a cup of coffee after sharing the morning chores in the ward.

'Well, to start with. . .' She got no further. There was a commotion in the corridor which brought both of them to their feet, and at that moment Toby Jenkins, one of the sports teachers, appeared in the doorway carrying Piers Bellamy in his arms.

'He's having an asthma attack,' said Toby. 'It seems to be a severe one.'

Piers was doubled up, clutching his abdomen and

breathing with difficulty, trying to shake his head from side to side. Clearly he couldn't speak.

Both Lucy and Ruth guided Toby to a chair.

'Sit him down here,' said Ruth.

'Doesn't look like a typical asthma attack,' said Lucy. 'What happened, Toby, how did it start?' she bent over the boy and began massaging his chest and abdomen very gently. 'Did he have a fall?'

'The kids were fooling about playing leapfrog before we started the match,' Toby explained. 'I let them, it's a good warm-up activity. Piers was jumping over someone and they both went down — they do it all the time. They both seemed OK until a few moments later when this lad suddenly doubled up and had breathing difficulties. I thought it must be one of his usual attacks, but I couldn't get him to use his inhaler.'

'I'm not surprised — he knows the difference between asthma and something else. He's winded, Toby, though it might precipitate an attack later.'

Toby pulled a face. 'Well, I'm damned! I've seen plenty of people winded, but it's usually directly after a blow on the solar plexus — there's not even a small gap.'

'Your attention was elsewhere, perhaps you didn't see it immediately, and, knowing Piers's history, assumed it was his asthma bothering him.'

'Fair enough, that's probably how it was.'

Piers was beginning to breathe easier and straighten up a little. 'That's why I. . .' he struggled to speak '. . .didn't want to use. . .ventilator,' he squeezed out.

'Quite right,' said Lucy, smiling at him and continuing to massage his abdomen. 'But you need to sit quietly for a bit, and keep warm, and we'll conjure you up something to drink in a little while. No more sports today, I'm afraid.'

'Then I might as well push off,' said Toby. He patted

the boy's shoulder. 'Sorry about this, old chap. See you.'

Ruth said, 'Toby, will you call in later to sign the accident book?'

He frowned. 'Lord, I'd forgotten that.' He dropped his voice. 'Do you think I'll get a rocket from His Nibs, our new MO, for letting his son and heir get into difficulties?'

Lucy hadn't thought about it and had a momentary pang of anxiety, but Ruth said at once, 'Of course not, he's a very understanding man and must know that these things can happen. He won't hold you responsible for this sort of accident.'

'Well, I just hope you're right,' said Toby doubtfully.

'Of course I am. Hadn't you better get back to the rest of your tribe before they start savaging each other?'

'I'm gone,' said Toby, and jogged away down the corridor.

Piers was somewhat improved by now, but complained of nausea. Lucy and Ruth helped him into the ward and made him comfortable, propped up on a bed with a towel and basin to hand.

'I'm going to let your father know what's happened, Piers,' said Lucy.

He pulled a face. 'Must you, Miss Shaw?' he asked. 'He gets rattled when any of us are a bit off.'

The thought of the doctor being 'rattled' by a small accident was as surprising as had been Hattie's remark about him being a 'poor lamb'. Neither description seemed to fit the spartan Hugh Bellamy, and even having experienced his gentleness first hand when she was ill didn't quite prepare her for his barely concealed concern for his son when he arrived about an hour later.

'How is he?' he asked Lucy as he strode through the

door of Matron's office, and both his voice and his manner betrayed his anxiety.

Hiding her surprise, but not able to hide her pleasure at seeing him, Lucy beamed. 'Oh, quite recovered from the winding,' she told him. 'As I explained when I phoned, I did so just to put you in the picture, not because there was any emergency, and we've only kept Piers in the san because he had a slight asthma attack following the incident. He really is fit enough to go back to class now.'

Hugh frowned, 'I'd like to have a look at him first, Miss Shaw,' and then added politely, 'If I may?'

'Of course, Doctor.' As if I'd refuse! thought Lucy as she led the way into the ward, disappointed to find him so unbending, though she had half expected it, realising that apprehension was making him seem more than usually formal.

He held the ward door open for her, but then strode past her in his eagerness to get to his son. Lucy found it endearing that such a normally composed man could display his feelings quite readily.

He reached the chair in which Piers was now sitting. Father and son smiled at each other, and the doctor's arctic-grey eyes became a soft, smoky bluish-grey. 'Hello, old chap, how are you feeling?'

'Fine,' said Piers without hesitation. 'I was only winded, you know.'

'Yes, Miss Shaw has told me, though I understand you had a mild attack afterwards.'

'It wasn't anything, Daddy, honestly. Was it, Miss Shaw?' Piers looked pleadingly at her.

'Almost nothing,' she confirmed.

'You two,' said the doctor, smiling broadly with relief, 'you two are giving me the run-around, I think.' To Lucy's surprise, he was almost twinkling.

'No, we're not, are we, Miss Shaw?' beseeched Piers.

'Certainly not,' said Lucy, crossing her fingers behind

her back and giving the doctor a severe look. 'We wouldn't dream of doing such a thing, would we, Piers?'

'Oh, no, Miss Shaw,' said Piers, a wide smile breaking across the usually serious little face.

Lucy was struck by his likeness to his father, with his grey eyes and patrician nose. She wanted to hug him, but knew that neither Bellamy would appreciate such a demonstration at this time.

'Hrrmph,' muttered the doctor, but he continued to smile. 'Now, Miss Shaw, I'm sure you have a lot to do. I can carry on here, if you want to get on.'

It was a polite way of telling her to get lost, but she didn't mind; she could see that they wanted to be alone together, and it was lovely to see the doctor in this gentle, almost teasing mood.

'Thank you,' she said, sounding grateful. 'I'm covering for Matron for a bit, and I've certainly plenty to do.'

They all smiled at each other and Lucy made her way back to the office.

Ten minutes later a still smiling Hugh appeared in the office doorway. 'I'm off now, Miss Shaw,' he said, and the smile reached his eyes, and softened the contours of his long, narrow face. 'Thank you for looking after Piers and for so quickly recognising his symptoms. He was grateful for not being pressed to use his ventilator unnecessarily.' He stepped further into the room and looked down at Lucy. His voice dropped. 'And I'm grateful. For the first time in a long while my children seem at ease, at one with themselves, and it's all down to Mill School and to you, Miss Lucy Shaw. Do you realise that? In the short while that they've been here, they've blossomed, and it's you who has made it happen. Do you know what Piers had to say about this little episode?' Lucy, dumb with surprise at his words and tone, shook her head. 'That he felt so safe when he saw you here. Quite a compliment from a small boy who until a short while ago was suspicious of almost everyone, isn't it?'

This time Lucy nodded; her mouth had gone dry and she felt the colour ebb and flow from her cheeks. Her breathing was shallow and ragged. His nearness was overwhelming, and his eyes, his lovely smoky grey eyes, were boring into hers. It didn't seem possible that anyone could have a voice that was so low and soft and husky.

For a timeless moment they drowned in each other's eyes. The room, and the space beyond the room, was deathly quiet, even their breathing seemed to have stopped. Then as if in slow motion, Hugh stretched out a hand and raised hers from the desk and brought it almost, but not quite, to his lips.

'Thank you, my dear,' he murmured, and squeezed her hand gently before placing it with infinite care back on the desk. Only then did he stand up straight and break the eye contact, raising his to look out of the window as a spattering of rain pinged against the panes. 'An April shower,' he said, 'following April sunshine.'

'Yes,' agreed Lucy in a breathy voice, dragging her eyes away from him and looking through the window too, and wondering if she had imagined a tremor in his deep voice. Her heart thumped painfully.

'Let's hope the holiday weather is more sunshine then showers. I like a late Easter, don't you? The weather is usually so much warmer and more settled.' This time his voice *did* waver, Lucy was sure of it.

It was amazing, but Hugh Bellamy was making small talk, babbling almost! But was this only in her imagination? Could such a cool sophisticated individual babble? Had he been affected as much as she by the strange, out-of-this-world experience of moments before? She raised her eyes and dared to look at him again. He returned her look, but now his eyes were veiled, neither icy nor gentle, just fathomless.

'Well, I must be off,' he said briskly, and turned to pick up his surgical case which he had placed just inside the door. 'Again my thanks.' He inclined his head in a stiffish sort of bow, turned on his heel and marched out of the room.

Lucy heard his feet receding down the corridor in long, measured strides, until he reached the outside door. She heard him open it, then close it quietly behind him.

'Goodbye, Dr Bellamy, goodbye,' she whispered softly to the empty office.

By mid-afternoon she had regained her composure, quelled the excitement that thinking about her encounter with Hugh Bellamy induced, and was ready to deal with class P3.

P3, notoriously difficult to handle, all now becoming individuals, with the boys particularly wanting to do their own thing. Lucy had already discovered that the more action required of them, the more she could keep their attention, so she was constantly devising activity play-acting.

Drama was held in the old gym hall, well away from the main building and not far from the end of the drive and Lucy's cottage. It had at one time been converted from a barn, and there was a small gallery running round the top, where once grain had been stored.

Lucy blew her whistle long and hard. The shouting, milling children came to a halt, and their voices died away as she stood just inside the door waiting to get their attention.

'Right,' she said when all was as silent as it was ever likely to be, 'today we're going to a jousting match. You know what a jousting match is?' One or two hands shot up. 'Vicky, you tell me.'

'Knights used to do it in the olden days, jousting. Two knights on horses galloped towards each other, pointing their spears at one another.'

'Not spears—lances,' one of the boys said in a scathing voice.

'All right, lances. But that's what they did, rushed at each other and tried to knock each other off their horses.'

'That's right,' confirmed Lucy. 'And what else happened?'

Eventually all the children became involved in telling their versions of a jousting match, even to one of the girls explaining that the ladies of the king's court gave favours of coloured ribbon or handkerchiefs to the knights whom they most fancied to win. All the boys made sick noises and pretended to die of embarrassment, till Lucy told them they wouldn't be sent to hunt dragons unless they had a number of ladies' favours to their credit. Even the brightest of them wasn't quite sure if this was true, and kept quiet.

There was further discussion, and Lucy insisted that everything should be in mime. 'No hockey sticks or other possible lethal weapons to represent lances will be used,' she said, firmly addressing some of the boys who were hell-bent on realism. 'Acting is about pretending so well that the audience believes that you've got a gun, or a chopper, or in this case a lance, to fight with. You must also make them believe you're galloping on a magnificent warhorse, with gold breastplates and decorated harness. Now let's divide up into groups, some of you can be the ladies and gentlemen on the balcony, pretend it's the king's pavilion; others can be heralds, and trumpeters, and of course knights. But you'll take it in turns to act different parts. Now, let's get sorted.'

'Do you think there might have been a physician in

attendance at these routs?' asked Hugh Bellamy's unmistakable voice from behind her back.

Lucy twirled round. She hadn't heard the gym-room door open, but that wasn't surprising, given the volume of noise that P3 had been making. But what was the doctor doing here? She understood he had the afternoon off. She struggled to regain the composure that she'd just succeeded in winning over her emotions of the morning, but it was very hard.

He stood in front of her looking even more handsome than usual, dressed obviously in casual clothes as befitted off-duty. Beautifully cut cord trousers were topped by a chunky cable-knit sweater in royal blue. Was it the blue of his sweater that coloured his eyes, or was he revealing again the gentler side of his nature that turned cold grey eyes into bluish-grey?

Hot on the heels of this question came another. Who had knitted him his gorgeous sweater? The equally gorgeous sexy Hattie, perhaps? You don't know that she's gorgeous, whispered an inner voice, just because her voice sounds. . .well, the way it sounds, like every men's ideal of voluptuous womanhood. The word voluptuous made her giggle, it was so old-fashioned, thirtiesish.

Hugh gave her a surprised and slightly hurt look. 'I amuse you?' he asked, chilly-voiced.

Lucy was distressed that she might have hurt his feelings. 'Oh, no, not at all, you're not in the least bit funny—it's just a word, something that I was thinking, that seemed funny.'

He smiled down at her, all chilliness gone. 'Want to share it with me, your funny word?'

Lucy shook her head. If she wasn't careful this morning's episode was going to repeat itself.

He continued to hold her mesmerised. 'One day, perhaps,' he said softly, 'you may share that quirky sense of humour with me?'

Lucy cleared her throat before replying. 'One day, perhaps,' she said.

'Good.' He looked round the noisy room. 'May I stay for a little while, please?'

'Of course, we welcome an audience.' They exchanged intimate, warm smiles, something that until this morning Lucy would not have thought possible.

The children were arguing noisily between themselves as to who should do what. Lucy, exerting all her self-control, made herself forget the doctor's presence, and intervened. 'You, you and you upstairs,' she instructed, picking out pairs of children hovering on the fringes of the crowd. 'You're the spectators for this round. You can cheer or boo as much as you like, and throw down favours as you wish.'

The half-dozen children rushed up the winding stair to the gallery. Lucy sorted out the children remaining on the ground floor into their working elements. 'Right, we can begin, on my whistle.' She blew a short blast, and all hell let loose. Horses and riders galloped noisily across the gym, accompanied by yells and shrieks and trumpet-blowing that would have done justice to a battlefield.

'I think you really do need a physician around, Miss Shaw,' said Hugh in an amused tone. 'Someone's bound to come to grief under the circumstances.'

'A sort of *Doctor in the House*,' she said sweetly.

'Precisely.' He grinned. 'No good doctor could pass this by,' he said. 'Think of all those battle injuries.'

Lucy couldn't help herself; his goodwill and cheerfulness were infectious. Her plans for presenting a pleasant but neutral face at their next meeting dissolved. She bubbled over with laughter and delight in his company, and just for the moment she didn't care if he noticed or not. Perhaps the presence of the children made her feel safe.

Hugh was delighted to have sparked off such animation. 'I should explain,' he said diffidently, 'what I'm doing here at this time.'

'Please do, I thought you had the afternoon off.' Lucy ran her eye over the children to check that they were all more or less where they should be.

Hugh embellished the truth a little to cover the fact that he had jumped at the chance of a return visit to the school. 'One of the children in this last batch of rubella sufferers has otitis media — Ruth phoned this afternoon after you'd left the san. As you know, a slight middle-ear infection isn't unusual after any other infection. I offered to bring up the necessary antibiotics so that treatment could be started this evening. It'll save someone a trip to the chemist and gives me an excuse for a walk on my afternoon off, and a reason for not getting stuck into clearing my jungle of a garden.'

And an excuse, he acknowledged to himself, looking down on Lucy's bobbed and gleaming bright brown hair, to glimpse you in passing.

'Have you been up to see Ruth yet?' she asked.

'No — I was distracted by this rumpus. I just had to investigate, it was so intriguing.'

'Do you mean you could hear us from the drive?' Lucy looked up at him in surprise.

Hugh grinned, his eyes crinkling at the corners in a most attractive manner. Lucy blinked and looked back at the children. 'You'd better believe it,' he said. 'Twenty kids with healthy lungs, what do you expect? What a marvellous way for them to let off steam. Lessons were never like this when I was a child. In those far-off halcyon days we got rid of our aggression on the rugby field or in the boxing ring.'

Lucy looked at him again, but this time with a horrified expression. 'Do you mean you boxed, at this age? How awful. It's a brutal sport.'

'Ah, but you must remember, my dear,' he said,

realising that he must sound ridiculously old, a condition that he didn't feel, 'in those far-off days it wasn't widely appreciated that head blows could perhaps cause lasting brain damage, it was just a manly thing for little boys to learn.' His lip curled at the corner. 'The art of self-defence.'

'And offence,' murmured Lucy.

'Yes, that too.' His voice was suddenly flat, sombre.

Perhaps he's thinking of how aggressive Piers was such a short time ago, thought Lucy.

But it wasn't that. Suddenly the room, with its horde of happy, screaming children and the lovely Lucy, depressed him. She was so full of life and laughter, so like and yet unlike his ex-wife, and his own feelings were so mixed. Seeing her with the children, in her bright green leggings and short sleeveless tunic scared him, for, except that she was tall and slender with curves in all the right places, she looked not much older than her pupils.

He had left her in Matron's office that morning, stunned by their eye-to-eye dialogue, but determined not to give way to this young woman's beauty and charisma. It hadn't taken long for his resolve to wear thin, which was why he was here now, but he had sought her out with some idea in his mind of steering clear of romantic involvement and nourishing an innocent friendship between them.

Looking at her now, though, so young and vibrant and lovely, this seemed unlikely. Even if she were willing, he wasn't sure he could cope with another beautiful woman in his life. He certainly couldn't repeat the experience that he'd had before, no way; his children deserved better than that. Anyway, too many factors were involved. For one thing, he had a dependent family and other commitments, responsibilities that he would never dream of shirking.

It was ludicrous, but he couldn't shake the feeling

from him that even a friendly relationship with Lucy would be difficult. They were too far apart in lifestyles to make it possible. For although Lucy had switched from acting, in all likelihood she still kept in contact with theatre people, with their extrovert approach to life and uninhibited displays of affection. In other words, she would enjoy the same social whirl his ex-wife did, with all the problems that that produced for a hard-working doctor.

He knew, even as these thoughts washed over him, that he was really being influenced by the amoral behaviour of his ex-wife. He knew too that it wasn't fair; there was nothing to link Lucy Shaw with his ex-wife, except her beauty. Perhaps that was what he was really afraid of.

'I must go,' he said so abruptly that Lucy couldn't conceal her surprise. He patted his pocket. 'I must take this up to Matron and collect my infants and whisk them back home for tea.' He gave her a sketchy salute and moved towards the door.

Lucy followed him out. She was hurt. She was damned if she was going to let him go like this, so abruptly, so suddenly cold and remote after behaving like a normal human being for a few minutes. She'd had enough of being understanding and forgiving, and she certainly couldn't live with the sort of ups and downs that Hugh Bellamy was capable of inflicting on her, even though their paths crossed only in a professional sense. How dared he stir her up the way he had this morning, and again a little while ago when he'd first come into the gym, and then, with the veiling of his eyes, change everything?

'Hugh wait,' she called, as he marched down the path to the drive. Anger made her forget herself and call him by his first name, and she didn't even notice.

Hugh did. He stopped dead in his tracks and turned slowly round to face her. He used every ounce of his considerable self-control to prevent the pleasure he had felt when she said his name from showing. His eyebrows arched into formidable triangles. 'Yes?' he asked, politely, tonelessly.

Lucy quailed. She hadn't given a thought to how he might react to her impulsive plea. She swallowed, and produced a half-smile. 'I just wondered why you left so abruptly. Did I say anything. . .?' This wasn't how she meant it to be. She had been angry when she'd called him back, and she reminded herself now that she had a right to be angry, it was no good giving in to this man with his wintry grey eyes and aloof demeanour. She took a deep breath. 'I——'

There was a screech of brakes and the roar of a powerful engine, and a red sports car zoomed between the pillars at the entrance to the drive.

'What the devil——?' began Hugh fiercely, as both he and Lucy turned and watched the low-slung monster growl up the drive at speed, totally ignoring the 'Slow—Children' sign. 'Bloody fool.' He took a few giant strides down the path, then stepped on to the edge of the drive and waved the vehicle down.

Lucy, heart in mouth, ran after him. 'Be careful,' she called.

The sports car slithered to a halt beside Hugh, who continued to stand rock-like a few feet from the car's near front wheel.

'I say,' said the driver, 'you all right? I didn't expect to meet anyone hanging around on the side of a lane like this.'

The speaker was hidden from Lucy by Hugh's large form, but she thought she recognised the voice. She reached the end of the path and peered round Hugh, staring in amazement at the sports car driver.

'Martin?' she called out, a question in her voice. 'Martin Lacey?'

The driver stood up and rested his backside against the driver's seat.

'Lucy — Lucy Shaw, by all that's wonderful! It *is* you. I was told I'd find you here, but I couldn't believe it.'

He vaulted over the low door and strode round the car, hands outstretched. 'Lucy.' He pulled her from where she had stopped half concealed by Hugh Bellamy, and held her at arm's length for a moment. 'Still as beautiful, with your lovely hair and those fabulous near-green eyes.' He pulled her unresisting into his arms and kissed her thoroughly, first on both cheeks and then on her mouth.

Lucy, for a moment excited by his arrival, forgot herself, but it didn't last. Within a minute she became conscious of Hugh Bellamy's presence, and struggled to free herself from Martin's embrace. Dishevelled but free at last she turned to the doctor.

'I'd like to introduce an old friend of mine,' she said, avoiding the doctor's eye. 'This is Martin Lacey, a producer of plays and films. We were students together, though Martin was senior to me, and has made quite a name for himself in theatre and television. Martin, this is Dr Hugh Bellamy, the school medical officer and our GP.'

The two men stood facing each other, the one tall, pepper-and-salt dark, and aristocratically handsome, the other shorter by several inches, but handsome too, in a blond, sturdy fasion. No two men could be more unalike physically, thought Lucy as she watched them shake hands warily, nor, from what she knew of both of them, temperamentally either.

CHAPTER SEVEN

THE two men shook hands, reluctantly on Hugh Bellamy's side. The air crackled with his anger.

'This is a drive to a school,' he said furiously. 'What the hell do you mean by driving up it like a madman — didn't you see the warning notices about children being about?'

Martin looked suitably chastened. 'No — sorry, old thing, I didn't see them. Anxious to get here to see Lucy, don't you know. Thought I was still in one of those funny little country lanes that seem to be scattered around everywhere. Won't happen again, promise.'

Hugh looked disgusted. He turned to Lucy. 'Perhaps you'd better explain to your ill-informed friend,' he grated, 'that this is the Sussex countryside, not the M1.' He turned, ready to walk up the drive. 'And we'd better cancel our meeting this evening, hadn't we? You'll obviously be too busy to discuss the Simpson child now that your friend has arrived.'

Lucy was cross. How dared he suggest that she would put personal before school matters and neglect an appointment?

She said haughtily, 'I wouldn't dream of letting anybody down, Doctor. Please tell your friends that I'll be happy to see them as arranged.'

Hugh looked surprised.

'Your secretary must have misinformed you if you thought you were to see the Simpsons. They asked me initially to discuss Lisa's problem with you, Miss Shaw; they're not due to come tonight. I'm sorry if you thought you were to meet the Simpsons.' He didn't look sorry, he was his usual stiff, formal self. 'It's only me you'll be inconveniencing, so don't give it another thought,' he added nastily.

Lucy was sure the entry in her appointments book said that the Simpsons themselves were due, but she must have been mistaken. It was a trivial matter, but another of those small errors that undermined her confidence where Hugh Bellamy was concerned. Surely Isabel Mottram had said that the doctor was bringing his friends to see her, not that he was seeing her on their behalf? She had thought how interesting it would be to see this enigmatic man with his friends; it had opened up the possibility of seeing Hugh Bellamy in a different light, not as a devoted father or reliable doctor but as a person in his own right. She had been looking forward to it immensely.

Lucy hoped her thoughts hadn't revealed themselves in her face. Both these men in their own ways were perceptive, and she had no desire that either should read her feelings.

Martin had been watching them both with interest, a rather smug smile on his cheerful, boyish face. 'I say, don't upset any arrangements on my account,' he said. 'I have to get back in time for the show this evening anyway. I just wanted to make contact with you, Lucy, and make sure I see plenty of you while I'm in this neck of the woods.' He beamed at her. 'And I must say I'm glad I have made contact. I can't wait to pick up from where we left off!' His look and words suggested that there was a hell of a lot to catch up on.

It was the sort of remark that Martin would make, as Lucy knew, but to Hugh it sounded as if this wretched man and Lucy were not only old friends, but had been very intimate friends. The idea made him angrier than ever, and anger — obvious anger — was something he thought he had mastered a long time ago.

Lucy said firmly, determined to keep her cool in

front of both men, 'I'll see you as arranged this evening, Dr Bellamy, my office, six o'clock.'

Hugh nodded. 'Right,' he said tersely, and then in an expressionless voice, 'Good afternoon, Mr Lacey. I do hope you enjoy your stay in our lovely county. Drive carefully.' With this parting shot, he turned as if to start up the drive to the main house, then turned again. 'By the way, Miss Shaw, you won't forget you've got a howling mob jousting like mad in there, will you?' He waved a hand at the barn, then strode away.

Lucy, who was just about to return to the gym, felt herself blushing with a mixture of fury and embarrassment. How could he? As if she had forgotten! They'd only been out of the place for a few minutes; the children probably hadn't even noticed that she'd gone.

Martin took her arm. 'Come on, old thing, I'm curious to see what that sarcastic bloke's on about. Sounds like a riot!' He marched her up the path to the building.

'It probably is by now,' said Lucy through clenched teeth. 'It's one of my action-packed drama classes.'

'Action-packed is certainly the word,' said Martin, grinning broadly, as they entered and came under fire from a fusillade of soft balls and bean-bags being hurled down from the gallery. Lucy was right, no one had missed her, nor when the lesson came to an end did they seem unduly surprised to find that Dr Bellamy had been replaced by a Mr Lacey.

To Lucy's pleased surprise, Martin was quite impressed by the children's response to the drama class. She had thought he might be scathing, but, apart from a bit of nonsense about encouraging cocky kids trying to be miniature Oliviers, he had applauded her efforts.

'I'll know where to come,' he said, just before leaving. 'To look for local talent, and not only the kids' variety—their drama teacher has a real flair for acting.'

'Don't exaggerate,' Lucy said, though she blushed with pleasure.

'I'm not, Lucy,' Martin said, putting his hands on her shoulders and swinging her round to face him squarely. 'You know I always thought you had real talent, and you look absolutely fabulous!' He stared into her eyes, then let his gaze scan her from top to toe. 'You're maturing,' he said quietly, 'and it suits you.'

It was a surprisingly genuine comment coming from the rather superficial Martin Lacey whom she used to know, Lucy thought as later she waved him off down the drive. A few years ago he would never have said anything with serious intent. In fact, in the past she had never known when to take him seriously, he used to toss compliments around so casually. It struck her again how very different he and Hugh Bellamy were, and, even if their first meeting hadn't got off to a disastrous start because of Martin's reckless driving, she doubted whether they would have hit it off.

Recalling that meeting reminded Lucy that she had an appointment with the doctor in half an hour's time. Time seemed to have flown since she'd dismissed P3 and taken Martin to the Gatehouse for tea.

It had been exciting and refreshing to talk of acting and theatre matters, a change from the more restricted life she had been leading over recent years. Martin was like a breath of fresh sea air, heady with stories of auditions and first nights and production nightmares— the world of the theatre on which Lucy had turned her back several years ago. She hadn't regretted it then, and she still didn't, but it was lovely, and deliciously irresponsible, to listen to Martin and have news of another way of life.

He would ring her, he said as he left, and fix up a date within the next few days. For Lucy, having anticipated a rather lonely time over the Easter holi-

FREE BOOKS!

FREE GIFTS!

Play the "Lucky 7" Slot Machine Game!

AND YOU COULD GET FREE BOOKS, A FREE CUDDLY TEDDY AND A SURPRISE GIFT!

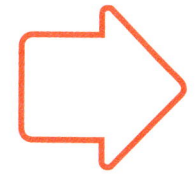

**NO COST! NO OBLIGATION TO BUY!
NO PURCHASE NECESSARY!**

**PLAY "LUCKY 7"
AND GET AS MANY AS SIX FREE GIFTS...**

HOW TO PLAY:

1 With a coin, carefully scratch off the silver box opposite. You will now be eligible to receive two or more FREE books, and possibly other gifts, depending on what is revealed beneath the scratch off area.

2 When you return this card, you'll receive specially selected Mills & Boon Romances. We'll send you the books and gifts you qualify for absolutely FREE, and at the same time we'll reserve you a subscription to our Reader Service.

3 If we don't hear from you within 10 days, we'll then send you four brand new Romances to read and enjoy every month for just £1.80 each, the same price as the books in the shops. There is no extra charge for postage and handling. There are no hidden extras.

4 When you join the Mills & Boon Reader Service, you'll also get our free monthly Newsletter, featuring author news, horoscopes, penfriends and competitions.

5 You are under no obligation, and may cancel or suspend your subscription at any time simply by writing to us.

You'll love your cuddly teddy. His brown eyes and cute face are sure to make you smile.

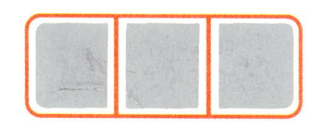

Play "Lucky 7"

Just scratch off the silver box with a coin.
Then check below to see which gifts you get.

YES! I have scratched off the silver box. Please send me all the gifts for which I qualify. I understand that I am under no obligation to purchase any books, as explained on the opposite page. I am over 18 years of age.

MS/MRS/MISS/MR _____ 6A3R

ADDRESS _____

_____

POSTCODE _____ SIGNATURE _____

7 7 7	**WORTH FOUR FREE BOOKS** **FREE TEDDY BEAR AND MYSTERY GIFT**
🔔 🔔 🔔	**WORTH FOUR FREE BOOKS** **AND MYSTERY GIFT**
🍒 🍒 🍒	**WORTH FOUR FREE BOOKS**
🍒 🔔 BAR	**WORTH TWO FREE BOOKS**

Offer closes 28th February 1994. The right is reserved to refuse an application and change the terms of this offer. One application per household. Overseas readers please write for details. Southern Africa write to Book Services International Ltd., Box 41654, Craighall, Transvaal 2024. Yoy may be mailed with offers from other reputable companies as a result of this application. Please tick box if you would prefer not to receive such offers ☐

MILLS & BOON "NO RISK" GUARANTEE

- You're not required to buy a single book!
- You must be completely satisfied or you may cancel at any time simply by writing to us. You will receive no more books, you'll have no further obligation.
- The free books and gifts you receive from this offer remain yours to keep no matter what you decide.

If offer details are missing, write to:
Mills & Boon Reader Service, P.O. Box 236, Croydon, Surrey CR9 9EL

Mills & Boon Reader Service
FREEPOST
P.O. Box 236
Croydon
Surrey
CR9 9EL

NO STAMP NEEDED

days, it opened up the promise of some outings with an amusing and easygoing companion.

She made her way up to her office just before six, conscious of the fact that Hugh had been in a ferocious mood when she'd parted from him that afternoon. Would he have calmed down? He had nearly always seemed sophisticated and severe to her, but until today she hadn't really seen him angry. It had been quite a surprising revelation, for although Martin's speedy driving had merited comment, it hadn't seemed to her to warrant such an attack from Hugh Bellamy. Well, she would just have to wait and see how he would react to her when they met. To add to that was his scathing remark about her getting it wrong about his appointment with her, as if she and or her secretary were dreadfully inefficient to have made such a mistake.

To her annoyance, she found when she sat down at her desk that her heart was still beating like mad at the thought of seeing this man. It was ridiculous! He hadn't behaved too well when Martin arrived, letting it show that he resented him apart from the driving, nor prior to that when he had left the gym so precipitately, so why was she feeling as if she was the one on trial? And why did Hugh still have this effect on her? Why was she still excited at the prospect of seeing him, when she'd just been entertaining a very presentable man, as eminent in his profession as the doctor was in his, and, more to the point, someone who had sought her out?

When a few minutes later, he entered her office, she knew why. She realised that he represented all that was strong and reliable in both a doctor and a man. He looked great, though he was wearing an out-of-date though beautifully cut tweedy suit. It was the kind of gear that Martin wouldn't be seen dead in, but then Martin, for all his theatrical presence, couldn't have carried it off as Hugh did, with his height and breadth and aristocratic bearing. To start with, he was unconscious of how he looked, and therefore not bothered by the impression he might make. Just as an hour or so earlier she had been uplifted by Martin's talk of the theatre, now Lucy felt herself being drawn into the more solid world of medicine because of this man's presence.

'I must apologise,' he said at once, 'for behaving so boorishly this afternoon. Your friend must have been angry.'

His phrasing might be quaint, she thought, but he means it, and it sounds just right coming from him.

'Oh, it's forgotten,' she said. 'Martin, for all his faults, doesn't bear grudges. He could see your point about driving like a maniac.'

'Good, you might pass my apologies on to him when you see him again.'

'I will.'

'You will be seeing him again, then?'

Lucy was surprised. 'Naturally—he's an old friend, and it will be fun meeting up with other old friends through him, in the acting world. I haven't had the opportunity over the last few years to do so, though I've kept in touch with a few. I'll have time during the holidays to see some of them.'

Was it her imagination, or did a hint of dismay pass over Hugh's face? She wasn't sure. Perhaps he was still concerned about losing his temper with Martin. He was probably angry with himself for his lack of control. She wanted to reassure him, take that pained look off his face. 'Anyway, as I said, Martin won't hold your telling him off about his mad driving against you. He knows he deserved it.'

She had an idea that she thought might please this cross-looking man opposite. 'Perhaps if you have a free evening over the next few weeks you could come and see what goes on backstage of the production that

Martin's doing at the Chichester theatre. I'm sure he'd love to show you round.'

The doctor's grey eyes, already bleak, somehow became even bleaker. He leaned forward over the desk and stared at Lucy. The nostrils of his fine patrician nose flared slightly. 'The very last thing I should want to do,' he said, through hardly moving lips, 'is visit the nether regions of a theatre. 'I. . .' He hesitated. 'I have no interest in the world of the theatre, at least not the professional world that your friend represents.'

Lucy's first reaction was to say, Don't be so stuffy, but she held it back. Her idea of helping this infuriating man to get back to normal had certainly misfired, but why?

She said gently, 'You seemed to approve of my drama training and the classes here.'

'That's quite different,' he said abruptly. 'You're putting your talent to good use, combining it with nursing, you have a splendid vocation before you helping those who will really benefit from both skills. But actors, acting as such. . .' A look of profound distaste crossed his stern features. 'They're butterflies, no staying power most of them, flirtatious, silly lot.'

'That's just not fair,' Lucy flared up in defence of her friends of the stage. 'You're either ridiculously old-fashioned or you've met all the wrong kinds of people in the profession. Because I can tell you that most of them are hard-working and as dedicated to their job as you are to yours.' The moment she had said it she wished it unsaid, not because she didn't mean it, but because of the look of pain and distress on Hugh's face. The fact that he was trying so hard to control it somehow made matters worse.

The room was deathly quiet, with only the ticking of the elegant ormolu clock emphasising the silence. They sat there looking at each other for what seemed an endless time. Hugh looked so deeply hurt, his eyes changed as she had seen them change before, from arctic to smoky grey. He swallowed, cleared his throat and said quietly, sounding quite defeated, Lucy thought,

'I'm sorry, that was quite unforgivable of me. You meant to be kind, and I've no right to say what I did about actors.' He managed to produce a smile. 'You're quite right, of course. The few that I met were not, I'm sure, representative of the profession. I'm so sorry, and it was refreshing to hear you defend your friends so soundly.' He relaxed a little and his smile widened. 'Am I forgiven, and may we start afresh and get down to the business that brought me here tonight?'

'Yes, of course.'

Abruptly he became his usual contained self, and Lucy wondered if she had imagined his less than usual sang-froid. 'Now, about the little Simpson girl. She's deaf, but not profoundly deaf, which is why her parents want her to attend a normal school. With some help, particularly from the staff, and understanding from the children, they hope to place her here in Mill School.'

'They think we can help her?' Lucy struggled to put all that had just happened behind her. If he could do it, so could she.

'Yes. The school has a reputation for teaching problem children, and now that you're here with your drama lessons, they're even more certain that this is the right place for Lisa.'

'Why didn't they come tonight to discuss this with me in person?'

'They've been disappointed before, and wanted me to sound out the position. It's amazing how many schools don't want to be involved with this sort of problem.'

'Well, we do,' said Lucy firmly. 'I believe the Frobishers would have welcomed a pupil like Lisa, and so shall I.'

Hugh smiled, the first nice uncomplicated smile of the evening. 'In that case,' he said, 'may I make an appointment for the Simpsons to see you as soon as possible?'

'Of course.'

They fixed for a time on the following day. When this had been arranged, Hugh said, 'Sorry there was a mix-up about this evening. I should have made it clear to your secretary that I was coming alone to discuss little Lisa Simpson.'

When he had gone, Lucy wondered whether he felt guilty about making such an issue of the matter. She checked the appointments book, which clearly stated that Mr and Mrs Simpson and Dr Bellamy were due that evening. How had the mistake arisen, and after how, why? If Hugh wanted to see her alone, why hadn't he simply said so? It was another little mystery that surrounded him, like the mystery of why he was so anti actors. Could that be something to do with his ex-wife? She had certainly played the social scene, according to the gossips, and many actors were involved with the upper echelons of the jet-set. Or maybe it had something to do with the elusive sexy Hattie, who, although Lucy had been at Mill School for a couple of months, she had not yet met.

The last few days of term before the Easter holidays were the happiest that Lucy had experienced since arriving at Mill School in February. It was virtually a triumphant end to her period of probation; her work during the rubella outbreak had been appreciated, and her continuing role as nurse and drama teacher seemed to convince everyone that her heart was in the school. It was wonderful to feel liked and welcomed.

On the personal front too, life had become fuller for Lucy with the arrival of Martin Lacey. His appearance that afternoon as she followed Hugh Bellamy from the gym couldn't have been better timed. Angry as she had been at Hugh's sudden change of manner, she might have said all sorts of things to him, had Martin not burst upon the scene and changed everything.

Later that same day, following the at first uncomfortable interview connected with little Lisa Simpson, Lucy and Hugh had come to terms of a sort, and parted amicably. The following day he had returned with the Simpsons, and everything had been fine.

Today he had called in at her office on the way back from the san. He seemed to be not dressed at all for an official visit; he was wearing a tailored blazer over pale grey trousers, a blue and white striped shirt, and a dark blue tie with a tiny gold motif. He looked even more stunning than usual. His grey-black hair and austere features made him look as always distinguished, but today the blazer gave him a casual air too. It's not fair that a man should have so much going for him, Lucy thought, as her heart gave a little lurch of pleasure when he entered the room.

He noted that she was eyeing his tie closely. 'My old hospital tie,' he said, fingering it.

'Yes, I thought it was. It looks splendid.'

'Does it?' He seemed pleased. 'I'm lunching with an old friend. We were at med school together, hence the tie. I haven't seen Pat for ages, and I thought she'd appreciate the gesture.'

Lucy hadn't thought herself capable of experiencing such a reaction to his words, but a shaft of pure jealousy and pure hatred, for that matter, for the unknown Pat seemed to pierce her through and through. It was much worse than the tentative feelings she had for Hattie with the throbbing voice, or Hugh's ex-wife. She gripped the side of he desk until her fingers went white. To think there was a woman out there who was not only lunching with Hugh, but for whom he was prepared to make a gesture! It didn't bear thinking about. It wasn't logical, but then nothing to do with her feelings for Hugh were logical.

'Did you call in for anything special?' Her voice was toneless, but she didn't care, didn't try to disguise it.

Hugh looked at her in surprise. 'Are you all right?'

'I'm fine.'

'Sure?'

For God's sake take yourself in hand, she muttered inwardly. She produced a weak smile for Hugh. 'Sorry, I'm rather spiky this morning—bit of a headache.' She forgot that only moments before she had declared that she felt fine.

'Oh, my dear, I am sorry, but not surprised—end of term and so on. Must be traumatic.' If Hugh noticed the reversal he didn't comment.

'I'll live,' she replied flatly. 'Now, what took you up to the sanatorium—we haven't got another outbreak of something, have we?'

'Heaven forbid! No, I was checking with Matron about medical stocks we'll need for the summer term. There are always a few hay fever subjects, kids with other pollen-induced allergies, and bites and stings, so antihistamines and nebulisers and such are the order of the day, and litres of hamamelis for bruises and sprains, and so on. Each season has its priorities, and I need to start ordering now.'

'You prescribed hamamelis for my hurt wrist when we first met,' Lucy reminded him.

Her anger had gone, as she remembered that first meeting and his kindness and encouragement. For a moment she just felt tired and sad, in spite of Martin's arrival on the school front and her generally uplifted spirits.

Hugh stood looking down at her. 'Yes,' he said softly, 'I remember, in the Copper Kettle in Chelchester. You were in shock. Clive had just given you the news of your inheritance.' He jingled some change in his pocket. 'I sought you out that day. I didn't go into the café by accident—I hoped you'd still be there.'

Lucy looked at him with wide and puzzled eyes. He was implying that he had wanted to get to know her before ever he'd found that she might be useful to him for his children. That was a surprise.

'I wanted to meet you after you fell into my arms in the vestibule of the solicitors' office,' he said simply. 'It was a bonus to discover what I did about you, and learn that we were to be near neighbours.' He put his hands on the desk and leaned towards her. 'It was the best thing that ever happened to me, Lucy—I promise you.'

They eyed each other across the desk. The wall clock whirred into life, overriding the classic restrained tones of the ormolu clock on the mantelpiece. Hugh gave it a startled look. 'Oh, lord,' he said abruptly, sounding reluctant, 'I have to meet George in ten minutes.'

'George?' Lucy queried.

'Pat's better half. He can't make it for lunch, so I'm having a drink with him first. We were all at med school together. They're a great team.'

Bells rang and cymbals crashed, and somehow she brought out the words. 'You'd better go, then, hadn't you?' She skipped round her desk and threw open the door. 'Go on, don't keep the poor man waiting.'

Hugh frowned. 'You sound as if you can't wait to be rid of me!'

'My dear Hugh, I just don't want you to have an accident trying to get to George on time.'

'Oh, he'll be all right, propping up the bar and chatting up the barmaid.'

'Then it sounds as if you should go and rescue the barmaid and protect Pat's interests.'

'Pat's quite capable of looking after her own interests—I told you, they're a great team.' Halfway through the door, he turned. 'Headache gone?' he asked, and looked thoughtful when Lucy nodded and said, 'Quite gone.'

'Well, I am pleased. Goodbye, my dear.'

'Goodbye, Hugh, enjoy your lunch date.'

It was two days later when Hugh got in touch with her again, though she'd seen his Range Rover go up the drive the previous day. Presumably he had further business to do with Ruth at the sanatorium, and as Lucy herself had done only a couple of short stints of nursing duty over those days she had missed him. With only a day left to the end of term, she was caught up in administrative duties, and discussions about timetables for the following term. Drama was now on the agenda, and Miss Tarrant seemed positively eager for room to be found for these lessons, following positive and encouraging feedback from parents.

Mill School was flourishing. From the summer term it would be almost full and have a waiting-list again — something that had briefly tailed off when the Frobishers died.

It was as Lucy was discussing this happy state of affairs with the headmistress and Mrs Mottram that Hugh rang, asking if he could call to see her. He didn't say for what reason.

His voice, even over the telephone, caused her tummy to churn with pleasure, but didn't on this occasion reduce her to a hopeless mess; she had Martin to thank for that. It was great to feel more on a one-to-one basis with him, so she was able to answer him naturally.

'That would be lovely, Hugh. There's a lot I want to talk to you about too.'

'Really? How very intriguing. Nice things, I hope?' His voice sounded warm and eager.

'Oh, very. Your children, for one thing, and their remarkable progress. I thought you'd like to have an interim report. It's too early for Miss Tarrant to give you a formal report on how they're doing, but I can speak quite freely.'

'You're very kind, Lucy. I appreciate the thought. Now, what time would be convenient for you? I have the evening off.'

A vision of him sitting comfortably in her parlour drinking coffee and liqueurs filled her mind. Would he turn the idea down as being too intimate if she asked him to her cottage? Well, there was only one way to find out, her new-found confidence told her.

'Why don't we make it a social evening? We haven't really had time to talk at any length since we both descended on Millweir, have we? Come to the Gatehouse at about seven-thirty and have a meal. It would be my thank-you for all your help during the rubella outbreak.'

There was a pause at the other end of the phone. Oh, God, she thought, I've blown it. Her heart plummeted.

'That would be splendid. I can't think of a nicer way to spend the evening. May I bring some wine?' Hugh sounded warm and eager.

'Please do,' she told him, letting her happiness reveal itself in her voice. She no longer felt the need to be guarded with him. A wonderful leap forward.

The day passed as planned. There were routine visits to make to all departments, then letters to do with Isabel, and staff meetings, endless staff meetings, especially now as the term drew to a close. Lucy was aware that her presence at many of these was not strictly necessary, but she either showed up out of a sense of duty, or because Miss Tarrant made a point of requesting her to do so. It was an olive branch that Lucy was only too pleased to grasp, knowing that Miss Tarrant now appreciated her more up-to-date angle on certain aspects of teaching children with problems—in fact, she looked to her for support.

This was still a novel experience for Lucy. All the senior staff seemed hell-bent on making her feel wanted and respected, a warming experience, she thought, but a time-consuming one. Never mind, she consoled herself, next term things would have settled down and she would be accepted but not overrated as she felt herself to be at the moment.

Because of a staff meeting, she didn't get away that evening until well after six. Hugh was due at seven-thirty. She had planned a leisurely bath with bags of time to prepare a meal and lay up the oval walnut table at the end of the sitting-room overlooking the walled garden, but she found she had to sacrifice the bath for a quick shower, in order to get everything ready on time.

She dressed in a peat-brown soft velvet dress with a waist-hugging wide gilt belt, tucked a creamy gold silk scarf into the unbuttoned shirt-like top, brushed her hair till it gleamed, and pushed her feet into gold kid slippers. She seldom wore much make-up, but tonight touched her eyelids with a smudge of palest green shadow to pick up the green in her hazel eyes, and applied the lightest trace of rose-red lipstick to her wide mouth.

'Well, it is your first proper date with the awesome Dr Bellamy,' she excused herself to her image in the mirror, and, pleased with what she saw, blew herself a kiss, then giggled like a schoolgirl. It wasn't so much nerves as joyous anticipation that was making her behave in such a bubbly fashion.

She had planned the meal with care while still in her office and reviewing in her mind's eye what she had in fridge and freezer. Avocado and chopped pineapple for starters, cold chicken, jacket potatoes popped into the microwave at the right time, with a tossed salad for the main dish, and a fresh fruit salad with whipped cream for dessert. Simple but elegant. Unless he was a vegetarian — oh, lord, what would she give him if he was? Cottage cheese, egg mayonnaise in place of the chicken?

Well, she would just have to wait and find out and rustle something up at the last minute if necessary. It was a practical illustration of how much easier she felt her role with Hugh to be, now that she could, without panicking, envisage preparing something for him at short notice. But she felt her pulses quicken and her heart begin to thump at the thought of seeing him soon, when the hands of the little ormolu clock on the mantelshelf stood at twenty-five past seven.

Refusing to give way to nerves, she stood back and examined the table set with plain but heavy silver cutlery on coffee-coloured crocheted covers disguising cork place mats. A silver matching cruet, cut-glass crystal tumblers and slender-stemmed wine glasses, all reflected in the shining walnut; with snow-white damask napkins clasped by a pair of tiny silver hands, beautifully worked and engraved, to complete each setting. A small posy of pansies and polyanthus provided a charming and colourful centrepiece.

She had debated with herself about candles, and decided that they would be too ornamental — too romantic? — for a first dinner party *à deux*. The softly shaded wall-lights were sufficiently welcoming, sufficiently subdued, without being too intimate.

In the kitchen she ground fresh coffee beans and spooned the powder into the percolator, to heat and bubble and reach perfection as they reached the end of the meal. Instantly the cottage was filled with the wonderful aroma of best Brazilian coffee.

At that moment the doorbell rang.

Lucy took five deep breaths, and waited for a moment for her heart to stop banging against her ribs and her cheeks to resume their normal colour, before going to answer the door.

When she opened it she was nearly dazzled by the orange-red glow of the setting sun, which beamed straight into her eyes. Hugh wasn't standing in the porch, but draped over the front gate looking across the school drive to the fields beyond.

He turned his head. 'Come and see this,' he said softly, and there was a smile in his voice which she couldn't see as his profile was in darkness against the light. 'In the top field over there.' He was looking past the hedge to the left at the long sweep of grass curving up the side of the hill. It was covered in short downland turf, and, clearly silhouetted against the skyline and the amber sky, there were two large hares, standing on their hind legs, boxing each other.

Hugh smiled at Lucy as she joined him by the gate, and this time she saw the smile and was almost as dazzled by that as by the sun. 'Hi,' he said very quietly. 'Isn't that wonderful? One hears about dancing hares, but so rarely sees them.'

'I thought they only did that in March—you know, mad March hares,' she said softly.

'It's spring in the air that does it, dear Lucy. I don't think they're particular as to month. "In the Spring a young man's fancy", and all that. And our four-footed friends seem as much affected as we two-legged males are.' His smile widened, his eyes gleaming as he turned to look at her again.

Lucy thought he might offer her a hand, or even put an arm round her shoulders, as they had to stand close together to look up the hill and the moment seemed right for it, but he didn't, and she realised he couldn't; his elbows were supported by the top bar of the gate, and his forearms were stretched out straight in front of him, and in each hand he held a bottle.

'My hands, you might say, are full,' he explained,

evidently reading her thoughts. His voice was rich with suppressed amusement and, she thought, tenderness. Where, she wondered, was the remote and recently, since the advent of Martin, rather angry man? It looked as though the perfect spring evening was working its magic on Hugh Bellamy.

They stayed for a few more minutes watching the boxing hares, until the sun suddenly dropped out of sight behind the hill and the animals disappeared into the dusky hedgerow.

'What a splendid way to start the evening!' Hugh said as they turned and walked up the short brick path to the porch door. 'A touch of magic, straight out of Lewis Carroll.'

'*Alice in Wonderland* or *Through the Looking-Glass*,' murmured Lucy, 'I can never remember. The Mad Hatter.'

'Wasn't he a rabbit? Not that it matters,' said Hugh. It's all a fairy-tale, and sometimes fairy-tales and reality run together in tandem.' He looked down at Lucy as they stepped into the narrow hallway. 'Don't you agree?'

'Yes,' breathed Lucy, 'I believe I do.' She thought she had a vague idea what he meant—surely that look in his eyes?

In the hall, the silk-shaded lamps glowed against the white paintwork. He smiled down at her. 'This,' he said, gesturing at the walls and sculpted ceiling with a bottle, 'is real, but it also has a fairytale quality; because of its kind it's perfect, an architectural gem, something brought into being by an artist.'

Lucy stared at him with her mouth slightly open, looking startled. No way had she ever thought to hear her visitor romance with words in this fashion. He was usually so down-to-earth, so factual, though he could be funny in a dry sort of way, especially with the children, but that seemed part of his professional persona. Recent events and her own sensible nature had enabled her to see past the rather austere man and doctor, but it hadn't prepared her for this. . .poetry. For a moment the saying 'high as a kite' flitted through her mind, that or. . .

'Poor Lucy, have I shocked or surprised you by talking nonsense? I'm not drunk or drugged, except by the beauty of the evening, and the spell cast by the boxing hares, and being in your company, and. . .' Even now, his tongue seemed to be running away from him in the most unlikely manner.

'And?' Lucy raised her eyes to his, and smiled. Whatever was making him so happy, she was pleased for him.

'Something rather splendid happened over at the rehabilitation unit at the County this afternoon—a little girl who hasn't spoken since she was involved in a terrible accident asked me to kiss her, just like that, out of the blue. It set the seal on today, it was bloody wonderful!'

He had surprised her again. She hadn't imagined it to be anything like this, she had expected it to be something personal. It was lovely to see him so relaxed, but it was also unexpected and out of character. Almost at once Lucy realised that she had no grounds for thinking this way, she didn't know him well enough to recognise when he was in or out of character. She might be in love with him, but she didn't *know* him. She'd caught glimpses of another man beneath the rather remote doctor, and the loving father, for instance, but nothing like this liberated, happy person. He looked years younger than usual, with a wide smile and his eyes full of light and laughter. She wanted to keep him that way.

'Do all your female patients ask you to kiss them, Doctor?' she asked in a teasing voice.

'Oh, certainly, all the time.'

Would he mind if she kissed him? He'd said that her company was contributing to his euphoria, but dared she go that far? He might feel she was taking advantage of his present light-heartedness, and regret it later if not immediately. As she looked hard at him in the confined space of the hall, she could see that in spite of his smile which wiped away some of the stern lines round his mouth, he looked tired. His skin, which had glowed healthily in the sunlight, on closer inspection looked pale, and his eyes were bright above telltale smudges of blue-grey.

'You're very tired,' she said softly, and touched his cheek with gentle fingers. 'Go and sit down and I'll bring you a sherry to drink while I potter for a few minutes in the kitchen.'

'Oh, Lucy, you're a gem, just like this perfect little cottage.' Lucy shook her head vigorously. 'But you are,' he continued, and bent swiftly to brush her lips with his. 'What shall I do with these?' He held up both bottles. 'One red, one white. I didn't know what would best complement the meal.'

'I'll put the white in the fridge; it'll be lovely with the chicken. The red?' She relieved him of both bottles.

'Save it for another time.' He leaned his broad shoulders against the wall, hands in pockets. In spite of being obviously exhausted, he still managed to look lean, lithe and handsome, Lucy thought.

She put her lips together in a firm straight line. She wouldn't let herself drown in those luminous grey eyes of his, not now, not at least until they'd eaten — all that work getting the meal ready. She almost laughed out loud. What a silly thought, how unromantic, as if that mattered a bean when this man whom she loved looked as if he might kiss her properly at any moment.

She knew, though, that it wasn't quite like that, not just her quirky sense of humour that made her put food before falling into his arms, but some deep-seated instinct that warned her that now was not the right time to declare feelings. If Hugh kissed her now it would be as much because he was tired and in a state of euphoria over many things — not just because of her. No way did she want him to say things to her without meaning them deep in his heart, and how could he do that in his present state? It would be like the classic example in reverse of a man getting a woman drunk for his own ends, if she took advantage of his condition and allowed him to kiss her.

He was looking at her now through half-closed eyes. They glittered through lowered, hooded lids. He really was terribly sexy, a quality that his usual remoteness generally concealed. She must get him into the parlour and herself into the kitchen before all her good resolutions fled. If she let him kiss her, she was finished.

'Hugh,' she said briskly, 'you go into the parlour, help yourself to a sherry and pour one for me, please — dry.' She started to edge past him, making for the kitchen. He didn't move. 'Hugh, please!' His drooping eyelids suddenly flicked open and he looked down at her in a surprised fashion.

'Lucy, my dear, I'm so sorry, unforgivable of me — I was cat-napping. Two sleepless nights in a row — can't stand the pace any more.'

Lucy just stared and stared at him. She didn't know whether to laugh or cry, then her duties as a hostess and her particular brand of humour came to her aid. 'Think nothing of it,' she said airily. 'All my guests drop off sooner or later. Go on, go and pour that sherry, a very large one for me, please.'

She escaped to the kitchen, ignoring his anguished, 'Lucy!' All those thoughts she'd had! Her cheeks burned. Thank God she hadn't succumbed and thrown herself into what she had thought would be his waiting arms — they would both have crashed to the floor. The thought made her laugh out loud, and then she couldn't stop laughing. She was still gulping and brushing tears from her cheeks when Hugh arrived with the sherry, which he placed carefully on the table.

He looked alarmed. 'Don't go hysterical on me, please. God, I feel so guilty. Lucy,' he took hold of her arms in a tight grip, 'stop it, dear girl, stop it.'

Lucy wiped her eyes and blew her nose hard. 'I'm not hysterical, Hugh, honestly I'm not—it was just so funny.'

'What, me falling asleep?'

'Yes—no, it was something else too.'

'Tell me.' He was beginning to relax. He smiled and released his grip on her arms but kept his hands lightly on her shoulders. 'Go on, tell me,' he repeated.

For one moment she was tempted. She was almost sure that he would appreciate the humour of the situation without being embarrassed or feeling trapped. Almost, but not quite. Better be on the safe side. She shook her head. 'No, not now, some day perhaps.'

'Ah, that sounds encouraging. There is going to be a "some day", is there, Lucy?'

Her insides went through all their usual motions of behaving like a demented food mixer as he spoke and pressed her shoulders with strong but gentle fingers. As always, he invested her name with a special quality, and surely that look in his eye spoke of more than friendship? She was practically back to square one with him, feeling vulnerable and defenceless. How stupid, after making such a good start, feeling on level terms with him, and even for a short while, in an advantageous position. Don't give in, play it cool, woman, play it cool, she commanded herself.

'Well, of course there is, Hugh. You're a parent, we're neighbours, without even trying we're going to meet pretty often.'

A closed look passed over his face for a moment.

'You know I didn't mean that,' he said, and his deep voice had a harsh edge to it.

'No, I understood what you meant, Hugh. I was just teasing.' Lucy couldn't keep the tenderness out of her voice. It was he who seemed vulnerable now, and she couldn't bear it.

He picked up both their glasses from the kitchen table and handed one to her. She was astonished to see that his hands were trembling very slightly. He raised his glass. 'Shall we,' he said quietly, 'start over again?'

Lucy raised her own glass. 'What a splendid idea,' she said, and lightly tapped her glass against his. 'Welcome to the Gatehouse, Dr Bellamy. I do hope you enjoy your supper.'

'Amen to that,' he said with a great deal of feeling. They smiled at each other over the rims of their glasses as Lucy took a large swallow, and Hugh drained his. 'Now what can I do to help?' he asked.

'Push the trolley through, please, while I pop the potatoes into the microwave. And pour yourself another sherry—you need it.'

'Yes, ma'am.' He saluted and wheeled the trolley away.

Lucy knew it was going to be all right; there would be no hang-ups, no embarrassment, they would have a lovely evening. She sighed with pleasure and hummed happily as she bustled about the kitchen. They had started over, as Hugh suggested, and he hadn't mentioned Martin as she rather feared he might. In fact he seemed to have forgotten, or was prepared to ignore, his existence. They would enjoy a companionable evening as good friends should, an evening that stretched before them with endless possibilities. An evening that had started off with a hint of magic couldn't possibly go wrong, could it?

CHAPTER EIGHT

MINUTES later the phone rang. Lucy answered it on the wall instrument in the kitchen. 'Yes, what? Oh, I'm so sorry—yes, of course, I'll hand you over.'

Hugh had appeared in the doorway. 'It's for you, something to do with a patient.' She handed him the receiver.

'Oh, no,' he groaned, and pulled a face. 'Sorry—I forgot to tell you I left your number to be used in an emergency.'

Lucy kept her hand over the mouthpiece. 'That's OK, but I thought you were off for the evening.'

'I am, my dear, except. . .'

'For emergencies.'

'Yep,' he nodded, and took the receiver from her. 'Dr Bellamy,' he said in his authoritative professional voice. Lucy could hear the distorted voice of the man at the other end of the phone. 'Can you get Sister Atkins to the phone, Mr Blunt? No, all right, tell Sister I'll be there,' he glanced at the clock on the wall, 'in about half an hour. And Mr Blunt, you stay with your wife and reassure her. I'm going to alert the ambulance and the hospital, just in case we need them.'

There was an explosion of sound from the other end and Hugh held the receiver away from his ear. When it ceased he said quietly but firmly, 'I promised I'll be there and I will, but you and your wife also promised that if anything was amiss she'd go into hospital. You needn't say anything to her at this moment, but I'm warning you that it might be necessary. Now, go and hold your wife's hand and help her with her relaxation.'

He put the phone down and looked at Lucy. 'I'm

sorry,' he said. 'This shouldn't have happened; Mrs Blunt isn't due for a fortnight.'

'Sit down,' said Lucy. 'Drink this when it's cool enough.' She placed a steaming mug of coffee in front of him. 'Black with sugar—it seems appropriate.'

'Smells wonderful! Just the job, thanks.' He took a small sip. 'I really haven't got time.' He made to stand up.

Lucy put a hand on his shoulder. 'Yes, you have,' she said, smiling but determined. 'If you don't drink that and have something to eat you'll keel over on the expectant mother, and what would that do for your reputation? Honestly, Hugh, think about it—a few more minutes isn't going to make the slightest difference, is it?'

He shook his head and smiled. 'No, you're right. I'll drink this, but I won't stay to eat, thank you.'

'I'm making you a chicken sandwich.' Lucy sliced into the breast of the chicken that she'd removed from the fridge, halved a large wholemeal catering roll, buttered it and slapped the slices of chicken between the halves before Hugh had the chance to protest further. 'You can carry on eating it in the car.'

He took another sip of his scalding coffee and accepted the roll which Lucy thrust into his hand. 'I'll drive you over to your surgery,' she said, 'and you can collect your case and whatever else you need, and I'll run you up to the Blunts'.'

'You can't do that, Lucy. I don't know how long I'll be. Give me a lift home so I can pick up my car. I won't let you do more.'

'Yes, you will, Hugh, because you know it's sensible. You're very tired and need all the strength you can muster to help your patient. You've only had a couple of sherries on an empty stomach, and you look a bit woozy.'

'But it's absurd, he protested. 'Once I get the old

adrenalin going I'll be fine. Medics thrive on too little sleep.'

'Yes, but they don't all have the kind of commitments that you have at home.' Lucy didn't really know if in fact he had to do much for his children, or if the sexy-voiced Hattie looked after them most of the time. She still knew little about Hattie and her role at the Old Rectory, she had been reluctant to pry, but she now had a legitimate reason to ask. 'What happens when you're called out at night, who stays with the children?'

'Mrs Trent — she's Donald Hubbard's house-keeper — comes over from the bungalow and stays the night when I'm on call, or as this evening when I plan to be out. She sleeps in her old room. It's a very satisfactory arrangement.'

While they were talking, Hugh finished his coffee and Lucy collected her car keys and a warm jacket, and changed her kid slippers for outdoor shoes.

'I'm ready to chauffeur you wherever you wish, sir.' She stood in the hall doorway and saluted smartly. 'You only have to say the word.' The soft lamplight fell on her smooth brown hair, her rose-red lips glistened as she smiled and her green-hazel eyes looked very green and full of laughter.

Hugh thought he had never seen anyone look so radiant, so devastatingly lovely. It was criminal that their first planned evening together had been spoiled by this call out. For once he resented his work and the unaccountable predilection of babies to arrive at inconvenient times. He swallowed a large mouthful of roll and returned Lucy's smile. 'I give in,' he said, and added in a most unlikely fashion, sounding more like a Martin Lacey than a Hugh Bellamy, 'Let's get this show on the road, lady!'

Lucy's garage was a converted woodshed outside the hedge surrounding the front garden of the cottage. As they walked round to it, Hugh remarked that he didn't know Lucy had a car. 'I've never seen you about in one,' he said.

'I only took delivery of a new one yesterday,' she explained. 'I couldn't afford to run a car before. Now. . .' She spread her hands to take in the cottage and fields and the school way up the drive. 'I still can't believe it at times, and it still frightens me, the responsibility of it all. I wake up in the night occasionally and wonder what the hell I'm doing here.'

'You're doing fine, Lucy, don't ever doubt it. I've every faith in you, and so have your staff.'

How quickly that evening they had slipped into calling each other by their Christian names, she thought, as she smiled a little uncertainly at his comforting words. He seemed to have shed his stiffness, and she her apprehension. Some of Martin's casual friendliness appeared to have rubbed off on her. Certainly the knowledge that Hugh still found her attractive bolstered her confidence.

She unlocked the double wooden doors of the garage and revealed her new, shiny bright yellow Mini.

Hugh examined it with a careful and humorous eye. 'Am I supposed to fit myself into that dolly's car?' he asked, grinning hugely.

'You'll find it very comfortable,' said Lucy indignantly. 'Look, I can adjust the passenger seat. There'll be plenty of room for your long legs.'

Hugh eased himself in. 'You're quite right,' he said, 'it is comfortable. It's a nice little thing, and it suits you.'

'I am glad that it meets with your approval,' Lucy retorted sarcastically. She patted the dashboard. 'Come on, Milly, do your stuff for the nice gentleman.' The engine sprang into life directly she switched on.

'Milly?' enquired Hugh as they turned out of the drive.

'My thoroughly modern Mini,' explained Lucy, wondering whether he would get the connection.

'Of course — what else?' Hugh beamed at her and sat back in the passenger seat, perfectly relaxed. He obviously didn't have a thing about women drivers.

'It's a bit unusual these days for babies to be born at home, isn't it?' Lucy asked as they bowled round the Green.

'It's coming back into favour, I'm glad to say, and provided that all's well during a pregnancy and there's no reason to suppose complications, having a baby at home is a rewarding experience. You need a good team, of course, a super midwife and a GP who's willing to supervise a home birth.'

'And you're willing, presumably, or did you inherit Mrs Blunt from Dr Hubbard?'

Hugh laughed. 'Quite the contrary — Donald wasn't at all keen, but then he hasn't been well for some time, whereas I jumped at the opportunity of delivering on my home patch so soon after coming to Millweir. I'd like to build up a practice where patients have been with me for years, and their children have been delivered by me. That's what general practice means as far as I'm concerned.'

'An old-fashioned GP, you mean, don't you?'

He looked slightly embarrassed. 'Yes, I suppose so. I suppose I'm saying that one day it would be nice to hear patients saying, "there goes old Dr Bellamy, he's a real family doctor, he brought me into the world".' His usually stern face was wreathed in smiles. 'God, I must sound a sentimental idiot.'

'No,' said Lucy, as she brought the Mini to a smooth halt in front of the Old Rectory. 'I think that's a lovely dream to have, and if only the medical profession realised it, it's the GPs that matter. They're the doctors who are there, day in and day out in the surgery. Most people know, or hope, that they won't need sophisticated surgery ever, but they'll have pains in their chest, or their children will get mumps or measles and need skilled attention. And most people would like to feel that their GP is also their friend.'

Hugh unfastened his seatbelt and turned to face her. He put a hand beneath her chin and looked down into her green-hazel eyes. 'Lucy,' he said softly, 'you are remarkable.'

In spite of the headway they had made that evening, Lucy was amazed that he should touch her face so tenderly, seem so prepared to let her see that he was not distant and austere.

Hugh cleared his throat. 'Lucy,' he said with a wide smile, 'you certainly know how to boost a man's ego.'

'A doctor's ego,' she said quickly, afraid she had divulged her deep, personal feelings.

'Whatever you say, Lucy. I'll try to live up to it.' His thumb travelled along her lips, and his eyes looked dark and unfathomable. She thought for a moment that he was going to kiss her, but he didn't. He sighed, then twisted away from her and opened the passenger door. 'I won't be long,' he said as he got out. He bent to look through the open window. 'Are you sure about this, Lucy, taking me to Willow Cottage? I'm now fit enough to drive myself, you know.'

'Oh, go and get whatever you need, Hugh—I want to take you, don't you understand that?'

'Yes, I do.' They stared at each other for a moment, hard.

'Then for goodness' sake go, man.'

Hugh grinned through the open window. 'OK,' he said. 'I know when to obey orders.'

A moment later he disappeared through the heavy oak door of the Old Rectory.

When they arrived at Willow Cottage, dusk had given way to night. A sliver of a new moon with a twinkling star nestling between the two bright horns hung above the cottage.

'Very appropriate,' said Hugh drily. 'A new moon and a star, what more could one want?'

'A new baby and a successful delivery,' suggested Lucy, handing him his surgical case from the back seat.

'As you say. Thanks, Lucy, for everything.'

'My pleasure.'

He paused at the window. 'Are you sure you won't come in?'

'Certainly not, unless I can do something useful. I don't want to sit in the kitchen for hours, boiling water—surely that's obligatory, isn't it?'

'Boiling water? Absolutely necessary for a good cup of tea.' His grey eyes were brilliant, full of suppressed humour. His earlier irritation at the interruption to the evening had quite gone and he was looking forward to playing his part in the new-life drama that was unfolding in the bedroom above the porch. Light was streaming out from there, and from the open front door. It all looked welcoming and peaceful at that moment.

'Isn't it strange,' Lucy had remarked on their short journey, 'that even hardened professionals experience a special joy at the birth of a baby?'

'Yes. You start off in a room with three or four people, and suddenly there's another living creature, a little mewling, wrinkled red-faced scrap of humanity. It's always unexpected for some reason, in spite of the fact that everyone's been sweating blood waiting for this little being to appear. I think this is especially true at a home delivery—the intimate surroundings, expectant relatives, all emphasise the fact that suddenly an extra personality is taking up space.'

Lucy laughed, he sounded so genuinely delighted with the idea. 'A very small space,' she said. 'A little baby weighing in at a few pounds.'

'It's easy to see you haven't done your midder

training. That little baby and its belongings fill not only the room, but half the house as well. You obviously haven't had anything to do with new infants.'

'No—only on the children's ward, but it's not the same thing. I was an only child and my parents hadn't many relatives, certainly none younger than I.' Her face, although she wasn't aware of it, saddened.

'Poor Lucy,' breathed Hugh, and touched her cheek gently.

'Hugh, don't for heaven's sake pity me—I've got, have had, so many good things—the most loving parents in the world for one thing, and many friends.' She nearly added that she now had his presence too, at the school, and perhaps, in the fullness of time, in her private life, but she didn't. In spite of the progress they had made this evening, she wasn't sure how he would react to that sort of remark. He'd let down some barriers, but the detached, impersonal man was still just beneath the surface.

'Go on,' she said sharply, 'or the baby will arrive without you.'

No prediction could have been more wrong. Lucy sat in the car for an hour, watching figures moving about in the room over the porch, thrown into silhouette against the thin cotton curtains pulled across the window. At last an elderly woman came out of the still open cottage door and made towards the car.

Lucy got out and went to meet her.

'How are things going?' she asked. 'Is everything all right?'

'Fine, but it'll be a while yet. I'm the Blunts' neighbour, Bet Withers—Mrs Withers. I'm a retired nurse and I've been trying to make myself useful. You're Miss Shaw, of course. Dr Bellamy asked me to come and have a word. And he said to tell you that there's some tea on the go, and would you like a cup?'

Lucy laughed. 'I get the message — tea and boiling water.'

'Well, the two rather do go together,' said Mrs Withers in a surprised voice, eyeing Lucy carefully.

'I can see I must explain,' said Lucy cheerfully, and proceeded to do so.

Bet Withers saw the joke. 'He's a nice man, isn't he, Dr Bellamy, even though he sometimes looks a bit forbidding?'

'A very nice man, and a good doctor. He's marvellous with the children at the school.'

'I can imagine. It's funny, he looks quite — well, haughty at times, and yet he isn't, not when it comes to patients. I think Millweir's lucky to have him. We need a good old-fashioned GP to take over from Dr Hubbard. His family have been here for yonks, but he's the last in the family.'

'I'm sure Dr Bellamy will make a worthy successor.'

'Yes,' Bet Withers looked her over carefully, 'I'm sure he will. They say he's marvellous with his own children too. Pity about that ex-wife of his — a proper madam, from what I hear.'

Lucy answered rather stiffly, not wanting to talk about Hugh to a near-stranger, 'Yes, so I believe.'

Mrs Withers was no fool, she could sense that Lucy was reluctant to discuss it. 'I didn't mean to put you on the spot. I just thought that as a close friend of the doctor's you might be better informed. There are so many rumours going around.'

The words 'a close friend' warmed Lucy's heart. That was exactly what she would like to be to Hugh at this moment in time, and perhaps it wasn't a too impossible dream, since the perceptive Mrs Withers had put her in that category.

'You haven't put me on the spot, Mrs Withers, but I really don't know anything of the doctor's affairs before he came here. I'm a newcomer myself, as you know, and the doctor and I simply met at Millweir. Dr Bellamy's concern is for his children, and he probably feels that the less said about the matter, the better for them.'

'Of course, and quite right too. Everyone's on his side, you know. The way the ex Mrs Bellamy carried on.' Bet raised her eyes heavenward.

Lucy wondered where she and anyone else in the village had got their information from. Surely Hugh's ex hadn't put in an appearance here? She had left him before he'd taken up his post at Millweir. She didn't have time to ask, however, for at that moment there came an unmistakable sound from the room above the porch; a new baby's cry, thin and reedy, but triumphant, or more likely, Lucy thought, shocked, or perhaps relieved at having completed its nine-month prison sentence.

She grinned at her thoughts, and Mrs Withers beamed at her. 'There's nothing like it, is there? A new baby, it does things to you. Even a tough old professional like me is inclined to go rather gooey. Ugh.' She pretended to shudder. 'Come on, let's go and break open the bottle of bubbly I brought over to celebrate.'

'What about the tea?'

'To hell with the tea, let's get this baby properly launched.'

I'm going to like Bet Withers, thought Lucy, as they walked into the brightly lit kitchen, she's got a great sense of humour and she reminds me of my own darling mother.

A few minutes later, while Lucy and Bet were still setting out glasses on a tray and opening a tin of shortbread — 'To soak up the champers a bit,' Bet had said — Hugh came down the narrow staircase that led straight into the kitchen.

He smiled at them both and gave them a nod of

satisfaction. 'A little boy, with all his bits and pieces intact. I've left Sister up there to do her special tidying up, and for Mum, Dad and son to get to know each other. We'll give them five minutes or so, and then pop the cork, Mrs Withers, will that be all right?'

'Fine, Doctor, just fine. Would you like a cup of tea while you're waiting for the bubbly? I know it's a poor substitute, but it's something to be going on with.'

'Ah, tea. Yes, please, if you ladies will join me. We've agreed that tea is essential to the process, haven't we, Lucy?'

He was teasing her about their conversation in the car. It pleased her that he should do this in front of a third person, as if he were emphasising their togetherness. 'Traditional perhaps, rather than essential — you know, the cup that cheers but does not inebriate seems appropriate to the occasion.' She said it lightly as if his remark had not been special, but her eyes flickered and met his for a moment and she knew he had read her thoughts.

Bet decided that the midwife and the Blunts would welcome a cup until the moment came for the champagne. 'Do you think it will be all right for me to go up, Doctor?' she asked Hugh.

'I'm sure it will be. Just give a shout, and I dare say Joan would welcome a hand to get things finished.'

Bet Withers flushed with pleasure. 'I don't want to be in the way,' she said.

'An old professional like you? Of course you won't be.' Hugh gave her what Lucy thought of as his special smile, and Bet almost bolted up the stairs with three steaming mugs.

'That was a nice thing to say.' Lucy felt grateful on Bet's behalf. 'Making her feel needed.'

Hugh hunched his shoulders, almost as if he would shrug off the compliment. 'Well, as to that, we all like to feel needed, don't we, all of us?' He looked intently at Lucy over the mug that he was holding in both hands. 'And it's a reciprocal thing, to feel needed and to feel someone else's need, isn't it?'

Lucy nodded very slightly, her eyes remained locked on to his. 'Yes,' she breathed. It was happening again just as it had before, this drowning sensation, the feeling that everything was receding.

The background noises of the kitchen, like the boiler throbbing and the clock ticking, and the muted sounds from upstairs faded, as she and Hugh stared at each through the steam curling up from their mugs of tea.

'Oh, Lucy,' he muttered thickly. The legs of his chair scraped loudly on the floor tiles as he stood up, breaking in on the intimate silence, but without shattering it.

Lucy stood up too. They walked round the table without losing eye contact. He stretched his hands out towards her; his shirt-sleeves were rolled up, and she noticed the dark hairs that curled up his forearms and glinted in the electric light, and the faint scent of soap and antiseptic that wafted from them as he took her hands and gently pulled her towards him.

'Halloo!' called Bet from the top of the stairs. 'We're all ready up here. Bring up the fizz!'

Hugh swore savagely, squeezed Lucy's hands so hard that they hurt and raised triangular eyebrows almost to his hairline. He gave her a comical grin. 'Full marks for timing, Mrs Withers,' he muttered.

Lucy giggled. She really couldn't help herself. This time they had both been in their right minds and in command, if such a state of euphoria could be right-minded, and still they'd been prevented from kissing. 'It's like a farce,' she spluttered to Hugh, who was looking at her with something like astonishment. 'A Whitehall farce, where every time something important is about to happen, somebody drops their trousers.'

He started to laugh with her, as she'd known he

would, his lean face creasing into rare lines of humour. He was a man who could laugh or at least smile a lot, she decided, and was quite sure she would see that side of him more often as they got to know each other better. It wouldn't just be glimpses of a gentle, humorous man beneath an austere façade, as had been vouchsafed her up till now, but a man relaxed enough to show his feelings to her. A man not inhibited by memories of an ex-wife who hadn't deserved him, who had left him almost demoralised and with the awesome task of bringing up three children.

She stepped back from him, picked up the tray of glasses and motioned to the fridge. 'The champagne,' she suggested, and started walking upstairs. His slow measured tread followed her, and she found it comforting and solid.

It was over an hour later when they drove away from Willow Cottage. Lucy had been introduced to Sister Joan Atkins, a nice homely woman in her forties, and to Mr and Mrs Blunt and their brand new baby boy, whose head everyone had enthusiastically wetted with Bet Withers' champagne. The baby was exactly as Hugh had described newborn infants to be — red, wrinkled and noisy in a subdued sucking and murmurous way.

The baby hadn't cried at all while they were all gathered round admiring him, just delicately gulped and snorted and dozed. There was no doubt about him being the centre of interest. Everyone bent over him and made silly noises, or in Hugh's case, traced the line of his chin with a long and, Lucy was sure, exploratory finger, as if even in these social circumstances he was assessing and confirming that all was well.

Once in the Mini, Hugh leaned back and closed his eyes. Now, thought Lucy, he looks exhausted, but in an exuberant, not defeated way.

'Talk to me, Lucy,' he begged, much to her surprise. She had thought he wanted to be quiet, to sleep, to take a cat-nap.

She said the first thing that came into her head as she drove down the long lane back towards the village.

'Why was Mrs Blunt so scared about going into hospital?'

'Because she had a baby just over a year ago—not here, but up north where they were living at the time. A perfectly normal baby. Mrs Blunt was admitted for twenty-four hours to have the infant. Just before she was due to be discharged, the baby was found to have an infection. Mother and baby were kept in for observation. The baby died of something he'd picked up in hospital—a rare thing to happen, but it did. The Blunts were determined this time that the baby should be born at home.'

'But why did you notify the ambulance and the maternity block at the hospital that Mrs Blunt might have to be admitted?'

'Because going into labour early was the one unusual feature of her pregnancy which has been carefully monitored. There was no obvious reason for it, except that some babies get impatient. But I had to play it safe. Thank God all was well, and young Adrian only wanted out of the uterus in a hell of a hurry.'

'How awful to lose a baby like that, so unexpectedly after it had been born perfectly well.'

His head jerked forward and in the near-darkness Lucy could feel his eyes on her. 'It's always awful, whether an infant aborts or miscarries or is stillborn. That's what I as a father, as a man, feel; God knows what a woman feels when such a tragedy occurs.' His voice was harsh, angry, yet only a moment before he'd been full of joy.

She took a hand from the wheel for a moment and laid it on his knee. 'I am so sorry, Hugh, I obviously said the wrong thing. I'd no idea that you felt so strongly. . .' Her voice trailed away.

Hugh lifted her hand and squeezed it between his and then brought it up to his lips and kissed her knuckles gently before returning it to the driving wheel. 'You weren't to know,' he said huskily.

Tears stung her eyes, and she had to blink to clear them. 'Is that why you're so keen on home deliveries?'

'Yes, partly. Giving birth seems to me to be a family affair.'

He was smiling, she could feel it in the dark. Thank goodness he had stopped sounding so sad. She could kick herself for having distressed him, however innocently, and it would be a rotten shame if, after all the ups and downs, the evening ended on a sour note.

She turned into the drive of the Old Rectory, and came to a halt with something of a flourish by the front door, sending up a spurt of gravel.

'Very neat,' he said, and the smile was in his voice. 'A bit showy, but very neat.'

Lucy reached up and switched on the courtesy light; some instinct told her that she would feel more comfortable with the light on. It had just dawned on her that they had arrived back at Hugh's home, and in spite of all that had happened, it wasn't much after midnight. If he had been driving and she was being dropped off, she would have been debating whether to ask him in for coffee or not. Would Hugh do this? She peeped sideways at him to see if she could find a clue in his face.

'Dilemma, isn't it?' he said with a chuckle. 'Will I or won't I, should I or shouldn't I? What would you have done, Lucy, if I'd run you home?'

Honesty, she decided, was the best policy. 'I don't know, really I can't tell you.'

'Well, that's fair enough. But I know what I want to do, have wanted to do all evening.' He undid his seatbelt and then leaned across and undid hers, and before she could think of protesting or pulling away from him, turned her face to his with one strong but at the same time gentle movement, and brushed her lips with his. 'Oh, Lucy.' His voice was fathoms deep and husky. 'Do you mind?'

'No.' Her own voice was little more than a whisper, a trembly whisper. 'No, I don't mind one bit.'

Hugh let out a huge sigh. 'Oh, my darling girl, you wonderful, wonderful girl.' His mouth came down to meet hers again, this time in a long lingering kiss, with his tongue gently pushing against her lips until she parted them and let him explore her mouth, and then fervently, with mounting excitement, she returned his passionate probing with her own tongue. Somehow, in the restricted confines of the Mini, they embraced each other with growing passion. His hands were inside her jacket, caressing and stroking until she moaned with pleasure.

She kept one hand behind his head, tangled in his thick hair, while the other found and unfastened the buttons of his shirt, and her fingers slid through the silky hairs on his chest and felt the strong, steady beat of his heart.

Lucy had no idea how much time had passed when she became aware of a tapping on the window. All she knew was that Hugh removed his mouth from hers, said something savagely under his breath, and in one smooth movement drew himself away from her and untangled his legs. 'It's Hattie,' he squeezed out between clenched teeth. 'What the hell is she doing here?' He wound down the window.

'Hugh, darling.' The throbbing, sexy voice seemed to fill the small car, accompanied by a whiff of expensive perfume. 'Oh—oops, I am sorry, I'd no idea.' She beamed a smile at Lucy. 'Sorry, love. The windows are all misty, I thought he was on his own.' She planted a kiss on Hugh's forehead, leaving a trail of vermilion lipstick above his right eyebrow. 'Darling, I do apologise for arriving at this hour. I was debating whether to ring or not when I saw this dinky little car and realised you were in it. What's happened to the Range Rover, sweetie?'

Hugh all but ground his teeth. 'Where's your key, Hattie?'

'I don't know, darling, I seem to have mislaid it.' She made a pout of regret with her glistening red lips. 'But listen, just let me have yours, and I'll let myself in as quiet as a mouse, and you can go on with—well, whatever it was you were going on with.'

Hugh opened the door with an explosive movement. 'Hattie, damn and blast you.' He turned to Lucy. 'I'll have to go, my dear—I am so sorry. I do apologise for this. I'll phone you tomorrow, if I may, and explain. And thank you so much for taking me to Willow Cottage, and for everything else tonight. Goodnight, Lucy.' He leaned over and kissed her softly on the mouth, before she could turn her head away, and reached for his case on the back seat.

Somehow she found her voice. 'Goodnight, Hugh.' She switched on the engine and sped away down the drive without looking back, buttoning her dress as she went, trying not to think, just concentrating on the drive back to the Gatehouse. But she couldn't blot out all her thoughts—the way Hugh had kissed her, the way his hands had explored her body, and she had let him! That was the most galling thought of all. That she had let him touch her in that intimate fashion because she had thought he...it was embarrassing even to think that his emotions were as involved as hers, while all the time there was Hattie.

He'd obviously been surprised by Hattie's arrival, and had been angry when she'd appeared, but clearly they were the closest of friends. Friends? Lovers, more like. She was beautiful in a wild, red-haired sort of way, and she shrieked woman of the world. They were so easy with each other, so sophisticated. If only Lucy hadn't let Hugh see the way she felt about him, it wouldn't be so bad. She could go away and lick her wounds in private, and put on a brave face for the world and even more importantly for herself. Now she would have to brazen it out with Hugh himself, pretend she was just as sophisticated as he. That murmuring all sorts of nonsense about love was nothing, just a simple way of having fun. Come to that, had she actually said 'I love you', and had he? There had been lots of darlings and sweethearts flying around, but the word 'love'. . . had either of them said that?

Fervently Lucy prayed that she hadn't; it would be so much easier to pretend that what happened was just a casual thing to round off the evening. After all, many of her friends from the past quite expected to end an evening out with their partner for the night. It was quite a common occurrence, and no doubt Hugh Bellamy with his greater age and experience found it almost obligatory to make love to the woman he had escorted for the evening. Or would he? She had no way of knowing. Perhaps he was a white knight in shining armour, as she had begun to see him. Perhaps he had kissed her passionately because he thought she expected it. Perhaps. . .

Her thoughts grew ever more bitter as she drove. She chastised herself. Sarcasm will get you nowhere, my girl. You can't blame him for taking advantage of you—he didn't, you went willingly enough into his arms. How could he know you didn't normally do this sort of thing? You don't go around with a placard on your chest saying, 'Keep off, I don't like being touched'. Anyway, that isn't true of him. I liked him touching me, I. . .

She had arrived at her cottage without being aware

of the fact. Automatically she garaged Milly and walked round the hedge and through the front gate. She stood there for a moment looking up at the dark mound of the hill, where only a few hours before, at the beginning of what had promised to be a delightful evening, the hares had boxed and danced, for their pleasure, hers and Hugh's.

CHAPTER NINE

THE following morning was hell. Lucy slept badly, rose early after her poor night's sleep and spent half an hour rescuing some of the remains from the previous night's uneaten meal and packing them into containers in the fridge. What she couldn't save she put out on the bird table, then carefully sorted the silver cutlery away into its baize-lined drawers in the elegant sideboard in the parlour.

'Well, so much for my first and probably last intimate dinner party,' she said fiercely to the wood ash in the now cold grate as she knelt before it and began to clean it out. 'Certainly the last with Hugh Bellamy.' She compressed her lips and let anger and disappointment wash over her. Her stomach felt knotted and hollow at the same time. Her mind was tired but would not stop turning over and over what had happened just before and just after Hattie had put in an appearance.

The awful thing was the woman had seemed quite friendly; had she herself been in such a position, returning to a lover and finding him in a compromising situation with another woman, Lucy knew she would have been furious. 'I would have scratched her eyes out,' she muttered fiercely, attacking the ashes so vigorously that they flew into the air and settled on her and the nearby furniture. 'Oh, damn, damn, damn.' Tears of frustration, and other emotions that she dared not quantify, trickled down her sooty cheeks.

It was her irrepressible sense of humour that came to her rescue. Her tears turned to a wobbly sort of laughter as she caught sight of herself in the elegant, mahogany-framed oval mirror that hung above the

Adam fireplace. 'Poor Cinders,' she said to her reflection. 'The ball ended at midnight, and here you are where you belong, down among the ashes.' This pantomimish thought sent her into a further gale of laughter mingled with tears, but after a moment or two she gathered herself together, blew her nose hard, and set about Hoovering and dusting.

An hour later, showered and fresh and wearing a primrose-coloured tracksuit, she jogged up the drive to school. The minibus passed her, with happy day-children's faces beaming out at her over the legend picked out in blue on the white sides of the bus — 'MILL SCHOOL, An Independent Boarding and Day School for Girls Aged 4-18 and Boys Aged 4-13. Tel. Millweir 811-536.'

My school, thought Lucy, waving to the children, soon it really will be my school. And I'm lucky, lucky, lucky. I mustn't let what happened last night spoil it, just because I let myself believe that a man like Hugh Bellamy could really fall for me in a big way. He was just being kind, and he was tired. Exhaustion makes people say and do unlikely things.

He said he'd followed you into the café in Chelchester, on the day you first met, an inner voice reminded her. So, a mature, handsome man likes the look of you. Heaven knows, that's happened before, you're not bad-looking. OK, she conceded to another inner voice, you're pretty good to look at. But that's not what men want, or not all they want, you've found that out often enough.

The bus came to a halt in front of the main house and the columned portico, just as Lucy puffed round the corner of the drive. Children were pouring down the steps of the bus, the three Bellamy children among them. Tess, the last to descend, stood on the top step and looked expectantly across the sweep of gravel to where the drive entered. She saw Lucy and waved and called out. 'I have a note for you, Miss Shaw.' She scrambled down the steps as Lucy approached. 'It's from Daddy,' she said, and handed Lucy a folded piece of paper. 'He said I was to give it to you directly I got to school. He was called out and didn't have time to put it in an envelope. His apologies for that.'

Lucy's heart bumped painfully. 'Well, you've delivered the message, Tess; mission completed. Thank you.' They smiled at each other.

What a lovely girl, thought Lucy, not for the first time. Her smile is like her father's. She pushed the thought away. Dangerous ground. 'Last but one day at school, looking forward to the holidays?' she asked Tess.

'Rather. We're going to Granny Lascelles for Easter, and staying over. She's got a pool and stables, and oh, it's lovely there.'

'Well, you know the pool here is always at the disposal of local children and anybody during the holidays. Do feel free to come whenever you like, won't you?'

'Thanks, Miss Shaw, but we'll be at Granny's almost all the Easter holidays.'

'Oh, well, that's fine. Have a nice holiday.'

'Thank you, we will.'

Tess was so sure that they would all enjoy being away at what was obviously their maternal grandmother's. Would Hugh be with them? Lucy wondered. Not all the time, surely; he couldn't take time off from his practice for three weeks, especially as he'd only just started at Millweir. Perhaps that was why Hattie had come back, to be there when the children were away. But no, Hugh wouldn't be so silly as to have another woman in the house when he was alone. This might be the nineteen-nineties, but villages like Millweir still had their standards, especially where the VIPs of the village hierarchy were concerned.

Mind spinning, trying to make sense of it all, Lucy let herself thankfully into her office, pleased to see that Isabel Mottram had not yet arrived. She stepped out of her jogging suit and re-dressed herself in a soft woollen skirt and russet-coloured angora jumper which she took from the cupboard. There wouldn't be time to read Hugh's note in peace. She would contain her curiosity and longing to know what he'd written, and read it later.

This morning she had to put in an appearance at assembly. She had been warned by Isabel and Miss Tarrant that she would be expected to make a speech on this penultimate day of term.

'It's no good on the last day,' they'd explained. 'The children are too excited, what with the service in the chapel and parents coming to fetch them.'

'What sort of thing do I have to say?' Lucy had asked Isabel.

'Oh, something about it having been a good term, with lots of good results in exams. Thank you for making new pupils feel at home, that sort of thing. And of course, you can say something about joining the school yourself, and how you feel about it.' Isabel had blushed at that point, presumably remembering her early opposition to Lucy. 'You could say that you're happy to be here and that we're like a family. And then wish them all a happy holiday and say that we're all looking forward to them coming back after the hols, and so on.'

'You make it sound easy.'

'I should think you'd find it easy, with all that acting training behind you.'

Yes, thought Lucy, standing up as the school song came to an end, apparently another tradition on the penultimate day of term, but half my audience is *behind* me, the most critical part.

She gathered her courage and drew herself up to her

full and not inconsiderable height, smiled down at the expectant, shuffling, coughing, and suddenly silent children, turned with a gracious inclination of her head to include the staff behind her, and began.

'Ladies and gentlemen, girls and boys — well, it's almost over, spring term. . .'

Once she had started it was easy enough, her nerves disappeared, and she talked clearly and easily, making the various points that Isabel Mottram had suggested, and adding a few of her own.

She returned to her seat after receiving a hearty round of applause. As she listened to the rest of the speeches, Hugh's note burned in her pocket. She both longed to read it and dreaded it. Why had he written anyway? He had said he would phone. Was he afraid Hattie would overhear? No, he could phone from his surgery or his car. Perhaps he was afraid that she, Lucy, wouldn't answer his call. The possibilities of why he should write rather than phone were endless. One thing, Lucy decided as assembly finished and she left the hall with Isabel on one side and Miss Tarrant on the other, she must get away for a few minutes to read what he had to say in peace and privacy.

She nodded and replied to remarks that both women were making as they all three left the assembly hall and walked along the corridor with children sweeping round them like water parting at the prow of a ship.

'Look,' she said suddenly, rather desperately breaking into the flow of conversation, 'I must go back to the lodge for half an hour; there are some things I want to do. I'll join everyone in the staffroom at ten-thirty for coffee, will that be in order?'

They both agreed readily enough, and with a great sigh of relief Lucy made her way across the entrance hall and let herself out of the front door.

The April sun glimmered out from behind a huge white cotton-wool cloud as she walked sedately down the drive, but there was little warmth in it, and her angora sweater barely kept out the chilly wind. If she'd had any sense, she'd have stopped off for her tracksuit. She jogged as soon as she was out of sight of the school windows, both to warm herself up and read Hugh's note as soon as possible.

The phone started to ring as she opened the front door. Could it be Hugh? She snatched up the receiver and said breathlessly, 'Millweir 811 245.'

'Lucy, you sound marvellous — all sexy and breathy.'

'Martin,' she swallowed her disappointment and tried to put a lift into her voice. 'How nice to hear from you.'

'Do you mean that, are you sure you're pleased to hear from me? You sound a little uncertain.' Even over the phone he was perceptive.

'Yes, I am, quite sure,' she said firmly, and knew it was true. She had recovered from that first moment of disappointment at finding that it was not Hugh on the phone. It was good to hear Martin's voice, and know she was talking to someone cheerful and uncomplicated, who could be relied on to stir her into lively action. Even when he queried whether she was pleased to hear from him, he'd sounded bantering rather than complaining.

'That's all right then, old thing. Look, I know it's short notice, but I can get away for a while this afternoon. I thought we might have tea together. Not really my scene, tea, but I want to see you, Lucy, even if it is only for a couple of hours. I've got to get back to the theatre later to meet some American types who are thinking of backing the show in the States. What about it, will you give it a whirl?'

Her first reaction was one of disappointment that he wasn't asking her out for the evening, her second that he was making an effort to see her, and he sounded as if he really wanted to. It gave her a nice warm feeling.

'I'd love to,' she said.
'Great, I'll pick you up about four, OK?'
'OK.'

She put the phone down and stared at it for a bit. What would she have done had it been Hugh ringing? Even the thought of that wretched man gave her palpitations, in spite of last night, and Hattie, and his general aloofness. Why on earth did she have to feel this way about him, when Martin was on the spot waiting to give her a good time? Whatever the future might hold for her, she was pretty sure that Hugh Bellamy would never play more than a fringe role in it. Except for the odd interlude of closeness, he had remained the enigmatic, remote person whom she had first met in Chelchester nearly three months ago. He was splendid with the patients, but generally concealed himself behind a barrier of cold restraint where she was concerned.

There had been those moments, though, in the kitchen of Willow Cottage and in the Mini in front of the Old Rectory, and that day in the gym before Martin arrived, when Hugh had shed his armour of remoteness. They had given her glimpses of another man, a man capable of warmth and friendliness, and even passion; but which was dominant, the gentle man so seldom revealed, or the frigid man hiding his hurt pride and heart?

She could do without that sort of on-off attitude. She sighed with sadness and frustration.

Martin's phone call and her roving thoughts had so distracted her that she'd almost forgotten Hugh's note. She fished it out of her pocket and read.

> My dear Lucy,
> So sorry about last night. What a disastrous end to what had started out to be an evening of magic, made up of dancing hares and other delights. Please

let me explain about Hattie. Tea, perhaps in Chelchester at the Copper Kettle, would seem appropriate. If I don't hear, I'll hope to see you there.

Hugh Bellamy.

Still, she noticed, the formality of his full name. Why couldn't he sometimes be relaxed and casual like Martin? Funny that both of them wanted to see her at teatime. Martin had readily admitted that afternoon tea was not really him, but Hugh apparently found the idea acceptable, and right for his image. Tea at the Savoy or the Copper Kettle in Chelchester would be all one with him, he wouldn't be fazed by either situation, but then neither would Martin if he cared enough.

Martin drew up outside the Gatehouse just before four o'clock. There was no mistaking the swish of his tyres or the screaming halt that he made in front of the cottage.

Lucy, putting the finishing touches to her toilette in her bedroom, looked out through the latticed windows. 'Come in,' she called. 'The front door's on the latch.'

Fleetingly, as he sauntered up the path, she wondered if she should have been so decisive about putting Hugh off because Martin had invited her out. She had left a terse message on his answering machine. 'This is Lucy. Sorry, I have another engagement this afternoon.'

Would he be hurt? A hidden desire to put him through some of her own pain made her hope so. It was at variance with her usual gentle concern for others, but she didn't have time to analyse it. Anyway, she consoled herself, the chances of it hurting the great Hugh Bellamy were remote in spite of their few tender moments. She had strayed accidentally into his orbit, but he had no real need of her. Because she was physically attractive, he'd been attracted. Well, plenty of other men had been before him, so what made him different? Because she was in love with him, that was what made him different. True love hadn't happened to her before, but now it had. She had known it for some time. She must face it squarely, head-on, and decide what to do. Love was the name of the game, and it hurt, but she mustn't let it ruin her life.

She recalled old Mr de Winter telling her to take her new life at Mill School one day at a time. She had, and it had worked. She had built upon each day until at last she had won the respect of the staff and the affection of the children.

Perhaps she should try to manage her feelings for Hugh in the same way. Meet each situation as it came, and trust to her instinct and good sense to cope with it. Yes, that was what she would do, she resolved, enjoy what each day had to offer and treat it accordingly. She would contact Hugh when she came back this evening and give him a chance to explain Hattie's presence in his home. That would give them a fresh start — who knew what might happen after that? Meanwhile she would enjoy Martin's company whenever he liked to share it with her.

Martin certainly wanted to share it with her on this occasion, and he made no secret of the fact. He came forward to meet her as she came down the stairs. 'You look stunning,' he said, taking both her hands and studying her carefully. 'Ravishing.'

'Hey, steady on,' replied Lucy, smiling with pleasure. 'Ravishing's a bit over the top, isn't it, for the middle of the afternoon?'

'I didn't know that sincere complimentary remarks had a time tag on them,' said a beaming Martin.

'Well, somehow ravishing sounds evening and a glamorous off-the-shoulder pure silk gown.'

'To me, honey-chile,' he drawled, 'at this moment it

means Lucy Shaw in a creamy cashmere sweater, showing off all her lovely curvy bits.'

'Well, you always did have good taste, Mr Lacey,' said Lucy, laughing at his extravagant praise, and loving it. 'Come on, my knight in shining armour, let's go and eat, I'm starving.'

Martin shook his head in mock ruefulness. 'There has to be a flaw, of course, in this beautiful creature. I'd forgotten your voracious appetite. All my other girlfriends just pick daintily at their food. No chance of you doing that, I suppose?'

'None whatever. Come on, let's get going.'

They continued laughing and joking as they drove through the narrow country lanes. Whether in deference to his passenger or because of his laid-back mood, Martin drove slowly and carefully, but it was not until they were nearly in the town that Lucy realised they were heading for Chelchester.

'I thought you were going to take me out for a cream tea,' she said. 'In one of those lovely thatched cottages dotted around.'

'Yes, I was, but somebody told me about this super place in Chelchester, the Copper Kettle, where they do scrumptious tea-cakes. Thought we might try it. Have you heard of it?'

Lucy took a deep breath. She hadn't thought to have her theories about taking things as they come tested quite so quickly. 'Oh, yes,' she said, struggling to stay calm. 'In fact, I've eaten there.'

'And is it as good as it's been cracked up to be?'

'Yes, it's lovely. Really olde-worlde without too much hype, and the tea-cakes are out of this world.'

'Good, then we'll enjoy our little feast together, Lucy, won't we?'

Gathering all her courage, putting out of her mind the picture of herself and Hugh taking tea there, Lucy replied, 'Of course, the Copper Kettle—here we come.'

They were lucky enough to find a parking space on the cobbled area nearly opposite the café.

Martin looked with interest at the buildings round the square. 'Nice little place, sort of Hansel and Gretelish,' he said.

'Yes, I've promised myself I'll really come and explore it one day, perhaps over the Easter holidays. I've so far not had much time, getting settled in at the school.'

The Copper Kettle was nearly full, but they found a table just vacated near the centre of the room. A waitress appeared almost at once, and Lucy recalled that the same thing had happened when Hugh had shared her table on that first occasion; as an attractive man he had been served very quickly. This waitress obviously thought Martin attractive and made no attempt to hide the fact. Like Hugh, Martin was unmoved by the attentiveness of the young woman. Like Hugh, he was used to being waited on by gullible females, thought Lucy wryly.

'Tell me about it—the school, your inheritance, everything,' said Martin after he had given their order. 'It's quite an intriguing story, rags to riches and all that.'

'How funny, that's what I thought, rags to riches.'

'Not surprising, really, that we both have a dramatic turn of phrase, since we both have theatre in our blood.'

Lucy shook her head. 'No, I don't, Martin. Nursing's my first love, and the classes I take are enough drama for me.'

Martin pulled a face, then blew her a kiss across the table. 'Dear heart,' he said, placing his hand over his own heart with a flourish. 'What a loss you are to the world of Thespis, all that beauty and talent wasted on a bunch of kids.'

At that moment Lucy became conscious of someone standing behind her, and without looking round she knew it was Hugh Bellamy. A hand was placed lightly on her shoulder — Hugh's hand.

'My dear Lucy,' he said in his deep voice. 'What a surprise, seeing you here.'

She made a huge effort not to show her feelings to either man, as she turned her head to look up at him. 'Hugh, how nice. Of course, you come into Chelchester to see your solicitors, don't you? It must be *very* convenient for you to have tea here, *alone* or even with a friend for a tête-à-tête.' Her voice was heavy with intended sarcasm, which at least helped her to overcome the treacherous wave of pleasure she experienced at his closeness. He would know she was referring to his invitation to tea, and she was suggesting that he had chosen the Copper Kettle for its convenience rather than for romantic reasons.

That'll show him, she thought triumphantly, childishly, then felt tears pricking at her eyelids. Perversely, knowing it had all the ingredients for a mini-disaster, she said brightly, 'Why don't you join us? You might have to wait ages for a table.'

Martin gave her an angry look and half shook his head. Hugh squeezed her shoulder gently. 'A kind thought, my dear, but not necessary. I have a table booked, you see, I thought I might be entertaining a friend, one of those tête-à-tête affairs, but my guest couldn't make it, but it seemed a shame to waste the reservation, and of course, as you point out, it is *so* convenient for my solicitors.'

She half turned her head again to look up at him, willing herself not to blush. He gave her and Martin a little ironic half bow and moved away.

Martin drew in a sharp breath. 'Well, I'm damned

glad that the man had the good sense not to take you up on your silly offer, Lucy. Whatever made you suggest it? An intimate threesome at our table is just not on.'

Lucy felt the blood come and go in her cheeks. She forced herself to say calmly, 'Oh, it just seemed unkind to send him away without tea—of course, I didn't know about his booked table.'

Martin, to do him credit, accepted her explanation. 'You're too kind-hearted for your own good,' he said, and reached across the table to touch her hand. 'You need someone to look after you, such as a selfish creature like me.' He grinned engagingly.

'Is that a proposal, Mr Lacey?' Lucy asked, trying to match his facetious manner.

'It could be, Lucy,' he replied, his voice suddenly low, serious, 'if you give me any encouragement.'

Lucy was amazed. To her Martin had always seemed the perennial bachelor, with a string of beautiful girl-friends in tow; now he seriously seemed to be suggesting marriage—it was unbelievable. She glanced away from him to where Hugh was sitting at a corner table. His back was towards her, and she was very conscious of his well cut grey striped suit, stretching across his broad shoulders. A snow-white shirt collar showed just above the collar of his jacket, and his neatly styled pepper-and-salt hair just cleared it, showing an inch of tanned neck.

She brought her gaze back to Martin, hoping all her pent-up emotion didn't show. There was a shrewd look in his blue eyes. 'Ah,' he said, 'so that's the way the land lies.' He shook his head. 'He's not for you, Lucy, a stuffed shirt like him with a caustic tongue.'

Lucy wanted to protest that what he said about Hugh wasn't true, but her innate honesty wouldn't let her. Hugh could be stuffy, and he was certainly caustic from time to time, but she knew there was another side to the infuriating man, and that with the right woman beside him, he might be the most perfect of men.

'He's not all bad,' she said mildly.

'You could have fooled me. Anyway, my sweet, I hope you'll give me a chance. I think we could have a lot going for us.'

'Yes,' said Lucy, 'so do I,' and meant it. She and Martin had much in common in spite of her having pursued nursing rather than acting, and at least he was straightforward and uncomplicated, whereas Hugh — well, would she ever really know Hugh even if he gave her the chance? Just because she was in love with him, there was no reason to suppose that, even if he were free of Hattie, he would feel the same about her.

'That's wonderful,' said Martin. 'Now, what about me picking you up tomorrow early afternoon and taking you over to the theatre for rehearsals and the evening performance?'

'Sorry, tomorrow's out — last day of term. Any time after that I can make myself free.'

'Right, the day after tomorrow. I don't want to lose any opportunity of seeing you, Lucy, and furthering our relationship. Does that surprise you?' He sounded absolutely sincere.

'Well, just a bit. It's a far cry from the old Martin that I knew.'

'We all have to grow up some time, and I just have,' he explained.

He really was a nice person, she thought, as a few minutes later they gathered up their things and left the café, but she couldn't resist a glance towards Hugh's table and his uncompromising back view. Somehow, to her active imagination, even his back registered distaste for her and her companion. She slipped an arm through Martin's. 'Come on,' she said, forcing a smile, 'drive me home.'

* * *

Lucy went through the next day like an automaton. She didn't think anybody noticed, not even Hugh when he came to collect the children after chapel on that last morning of term. By tradition, it seemed, the Frobishers had always stood at the chapel door with the rector, who came from the village to take the service, to wish everybody goodbye and a happy holiday. Miss Tarrant had suggested that Lucy did the same, and she was there saying her farewells to the children and their parents when Hugh drove up and stopped outside the chapel.

He strode up the path, and Lucy was aware of him as she wished the Halloran family goodbye. Her heart performed all its usual gyrations as he approached, thumping so hard that she couldn't believe that those nearby didn't hear it.

Hugh said a general good morning to everyone gathered at the chapel door, then apologised to the rector for not attending the service. 'Looking after my flock, you might say, rector,' he explained with one of his rare smiles. 'But I hope to make evensong on Sunday after I've delivered my infants to their grandmother. I'm taking them the day after tomorrow, but returning myself on Sunday.'

At that moment his 'infants' appeared, and, with goodbyes and thank-yous to all and sundry, the Bellamy family was swept down the path and into the Range Rover, by their father.

So he's not going to stay at his ex-in-laws' for Easter, Lucy thought, dutifully continuing to shake hands and wish everyone well in an automatic fashion. Will Hattie stay on, wait for his return? It was dreadful not to know, dreadful to think of her sharing Hugh's empty house, dreadful to think of her sharing his. . . No, she told herself firmly, I won't let myself think of that.

Somehow she got through the rest of the day, said her goodbyes and thanks to the staff, though some would be remaining in their cottages over the holidays and she would meet them as neighbours.

She was grateful for the moutain of paperwork that awaited her in her office, to be tackled over the first few days of the holiday, and she set about some of it that evening to keep herself occupied. Isabel Mottram had tried to dissuade her, reminding her that she would only be away over the next few days and the holiday weekend, and they could start work on it on Tuesday. To this suggestion Lucy, to cover her eagerness to work, quoted the old proverb. 'What you can do today, don't put off till tomorrow,' and to that added brightly, 'And I'm going to play hookey tomorrow, Isabel, and take the afternoon off.'

'I'm very glad to hear it,' said Isabel. 'You've worked so hard this term, you need a break.' With that, wishing Lucy a happy Easter, she took herself off, and Lucy was left alone in the empty school.

The following day she stood by her garden gate, soaking up the spring sunshine as she waited for Martin to arrive and whisk her off to his theatre. She was trying very hard to look forward to her outing, put into practice the idea of taking each day as it came and enjoying it, but her heart felt like lead. She hadn't slept well, her troubled thoughts of Hugh, Hattie and occasionally Martin keeping her awake till the small hours. But she had made up and dressed carefully for Martin, and the shadows beneath her hazel eyes made them look more green, more glowing. With luck she would be able to deceive even the perceptive Martin that she was enjoying herself.

It was very quiet and she heard his car coming from some way off. Then it turned into the lane — too fast, she thought, as it slewed round to enter the drive. She stood like a statue at her gate, and saw it hit first one pillar and then the other as it ricocheted from side to side. There was the sound of something tearing apart, a metal something, and a hot metallic smell soon after, then a terrible noise, compounded of many things, an engine racing madly, a human voice, distorted, shouting, glass, breaking glass. And then silence, profound silence.

Lucy froze at the gate, her head turned to look at the end of the drive. She licked her lips, which had suddenly gone dry, then turned and pelted down the short distance to where the car lay buckled and jammed against one pillar.

'No!' she shouted as she ran. 'No.' The word seemed to echo round the empty landscape and be swallowed up in the cluster of trees at the drive entrance. She didn't know why she had shouted, the word had simply been torn from her.

There wasn't a soul about. The car, Martin's car, was at an angle almost blocking the gateway, the rear end wedged into the massive stone pillar, the radiator and front of the bonnet crushed in mostly on the driver's side where it had hit the other pillar before slewing round. She stopped a few feet away, took deep breaths and tried to think straight. Martin's bright, fair head, Lucy noted with the peculiar attention to detail that sometimes went with shock, was luckily not through the driving window, but resting against it. She moved closer. Perhaps he wasn't badly hurt, perhaps he'd just fainted from shock, or was temporarily knocked out, perhaps. . . She reached the car, leaned over the passenger door and put out a tentative hand. The radio suddenly blared out in a deafening roar of pop music. She jumped and stepped back, then recovered herself and leaned in to switch off the radio. It wouldn't budge at first, but then suddenly responded. She was grateful for the comparative silence.

She climbed into the passenger seat and put a hand on Martin's shoulder. There was no blood anywhere that she could see. A memory of someone saying that the engine should always be turned off in a crashed car in case of. . . Fire, petrol leaking.

'Martin,' she said softly, 'I'm going to switch off the ignition.'

The key was hard to find just by touch, hidden beneath his bent body, and when she put her fingers round it it felt slippery and wet. With difficulty she turned it into the off position and removed it. She began drawing her hand back carefully, so as not to touch and perhaps hurt him. He must be bruised after being thrown about as he hit the gate pillars. But why didn't he groan or something? Because he was. . . An icy chill ran up and down her back. She stayed where she was with her hand and arm half withdrawn from between his doubled-up form and the dashboard. Her lips framed the word *dead*, but no sound came out. She must take his pulse. She couldn't see either wrist, they were both hidden by the way he was slumped over the wheel. The fingers of her free hand, steady now that she had found something constructive to do, found his temporal pulse, and felt a faint erratic beat. How deeply unconscious is he? she wondered. He might hear me if I speak.

'Martin, it's Lucy, can you hear me?' Absolutely no response, not the slightest flutter of movement. Slowly she began easing her trapped hand, clasping the ignition key, from beneath him. Mustn't move him, she remembered from her casualty lectures, might have a stove-in chest wound, safer to leave him as he was till medical help available. Help! 'Martin, I'm going for help. I'll not be long.' Her hand at last came free. It was heavily smeared with blood, so was the ignition key. She stared at her bloodstained hand and key.

'Don't move him at all,' said a firm authoritative voice, Hugh's voice. 'Leave him where he is.'

Lucy gaped at Hugh, who seemed to have materialised soundlessly and now stood opposite her on the driver's side of the car. She was never so pleased to see anyone in her life. 'Hugh, thank God. . .'

'That I was passing,' he said briskly. 'Now, Lucy, slowly slide yourself out of the passenger seat so I can get in.' He walked round the car. 'Chest wound, do you think?' he asked as he slid into the seat she had vacated.

'Yes, a possible stove-in chest.'

'Certainly looks possible; these old cars don't have the built-in safety factors of new ones.' He was doing as he spoke exactly what Lucy had done, taking Martin's temporal pulse. 'Pretty poor,' he said. He lifted the injured man's eyelids and shone a pencil of light into them from the torch he removed from his top pocket. 'Nothing much we can do without help. Use my car phone and get an ambulance and police — you know the drill, let them know there's a suspected steering-wheel injury.'

Lucy nodded. She squeezed herself round the front of the long, low-slung sports car, out through the wrought-iron gates secured permanently back to the pillars, and crossed to Hugh's Range Rover drawn up on the verge of the lane. A milk float was creeping down the lane from the other direction. Lucy made signs that brought the driver to a standstill at a point where he could see the entrance to the school drive.

'Strewth!' he exclaimed. 'What's happened?'

'Accident. I'm phoning for an ambulance,' she waved the small hand instrument at him. 'Will you pull up at the bottom of the lane and prevent anyone tearing up?'

'Sure thing — yes, sure. But can I do anything here?'

'No. Dr Bellamy's there with the driver.'

'Right, I'll go down by the Green, then.' The milk float hummed jerkily away down the lane.

Lucy was surprised at how quickly she got through

to the ambulance service and passed on her message. The operator told her he would notify the police. The minute she had finished, she rushed back to the battered car.

'How is he?' she asked as she reached it. 'Has he come round? Poor dear Martin.' She swallowed tears that were a mixture of shock and anxiety, and even in that moment thought how ironic it was that Hugh, who had told Martin off about his driving, should be the doctor on the spot giving him aid.

'No, but he probably will soon, and when he does he'll need something to counteract the pain. I'll give him a shot of morphine or something. We won't really know the extent of this chest wound until we move him off the wheel, but I don't want to do that until the ambulance people arrive, let's hope with a medic or paramedic on board. They're the experts in this sort of thing. If the wound has penetrated the chest wall, he may be in trouble with a lung puncture, as you well know.'

Lucy knew he was talking to her as a professional to help her cope with this personal tragedy. She struggled to respond calmly. 'Let's hope he comes round soon.'

As if on cue, Martin groaned and tried to raise his head. 'Stay put,' said Hugh. 'Don't try to move. You've had an accident in your car, but an ambulance is on the way, and we don't want to move you till then.'

In spite of being told not to move, Martin raised his head slightly, saw Lucy and frowned. His lips moved. 'Lucy?'

'I'm here, Martin. Look, do as Hugh says, don't try to move.' She stroked his fair hair back from his temples with gentle fingers. 'Do you hurt anywhere particularly, love?'

'Chest—feels like a lump. Can't you sit me up?'

'No, sorry, old chap,' said Hugh softly. 'We'll do that when we have more help; do more harm than good to move you yet. The ambulance people will have equipment on board and get you to hospital quickly, but I'm going to give you something for the pain.' He rummaged in his case and then held up a vial which he showed to Lucy. 'Pethilorfan,' he said. 'Should do the trick.' He searched his case again and came up with a pair of stitch scissors. 'Can you cut a small hole in his trouser leg, Lucy? I'm going to give him the injection in front of thigh—the most accessible point, I think.'

Lucy did what was necessary and Hugh neatly injected the painkilling drug. As he finished, they heard the sound of the ambulance approaching, followed by a police car. The police were just in time to take control of the small crowd of villagers who had begun to collect, and organise the cars coming down the lane from the other direction.

Hugh had a conversation with the ambulance doctor, and together they examined Martin, listening carefully to the back of his chest through their stethoscopes. Lucy stayed in her crouched-down position, stroking Martin's forehead to let him know that she was still there, although he appeared to have slipped into unconsciousness again, whether on account of his injuries or the injection she wasn't sure.

She felt a hand on her shoulder. It was Hugh. He said gently, 'It sounds like a lung puncture, Lucy. They're going to ease him off the wheel and apply a pressure pad to the wound as soon as they can get at it. There won't be room for you in the ambulance, so we'll follow along in my car.'

'All right,' she said wearily, past arguing. For some reason she thought she should drive herself, but to have Hugh's solid comforting person beside her as they followed the ambulance was too tempting. There was no reason for her to feel disloyal to Martin for accepting Hugh's offer, especially ridiculous considering what he had already done for him, if not saving his life, certainly easing his pain. But the one was a medical matter; driving her to the hospital was personal, outside his duties. Surely, though, it was nothing special; he would do the same for any acquaintance who had suffered a shock because a friend had been seriously injured. She must not read anything significant into Hugh's offer, and nobody, not even the ebullient Hattie, could make anything of such a mercy mission, and the generous Martin would be grateful that she had Hugh's support.

She sighed heavily as she seated herself in the Range Rover and fastened her seatbelt.

'Close your eyes and try to have a doze,' suggested Hugh as they followed the ambulance down the lane. 'You look tired, as if you didn't sleep well, quite apart from the shock you've just had.' His eyes were on the road so she couldn't tell if he was being sarcastic, just stating the obvious, or concerned.

Trust him to notice that she hadn't slept well. Much good it had done her, putting on careful make-up — Hugh had seen through it in an instant. She wanted to think only about Martin and will him not to be too badly hurt, but somehow she couldn't control her rambling thoughts. She supposed it was shock making her think of trivial things when she should have been concentrating on Martin's condition.

Poor dear Martin — she fixed her gaze on the ambulance cruising in front of them. 'Please God,' she whispered, 'let him not die. I'll marry him if that's what he wants.'

Hugh glanced quickly at her. 'He's in good hands,' he said softly. 'He's got every chance, you know that as well as I do.'

The ambulance turned into the hospital complex, came to a halt and was met by staff from the casualty department. Hugh followed closely behind, as Martin was wheeled into the building on a stretcher.

'Come on, my dear, let's go.' Hugh was standing by the opened passenger door. He unfastened Lucy's seatbelt and almost lifted her down. 'Come on, let's see if we can do anything to help.' He tucked her nerveless arm under his and escorted her into the accident reception area.

CHAPTER TEN

THE next few days—indeed, the next few weeks extending over the Easter holidays and beyond—were, for Lucy, a time of trial and assessment and a personal bittersweet agony where Hugh was concerned.

Martin remained gravely ill for nearly two weeks. His unconsciousness had persisted for a week; the doctors called it a stupor, which as Lucy knew meant that he could be roused, albeit briefly, so he was only superficially unconscious. They couldn't be sure, and wouldn't be definite about whether there was likely to be any brain damage. They took all sorts of X-rays, brain scans and blood-tests, and made one discovery, that he was an epileptic.

'Possibly the cause of his accident,' suggested one doctor to Lucy. 'A *petit* or a *grand mal*. These fits associated with epilepsy can be sudden, especially for people who don't know they have the disease. Once he's fit enough to be told of his condition he'll be able to recognise some of the signs and take precautions. But then, as a nurse, you know all this.' He was, like most of the staff, kind and understanding, realising that in spite of her professional knowledge Lucy's personal involvement made her need the same support that any close relative or friend might need.

Only one doctor seemed to be lacking in sympathy, a youngish, rather overbearing registrar, who told Lucy baldly, 'We don't think there'll be much if any cerebral damage, but only time will tell.'

He seemed much too casual, too dismissive of the possibility that Martin might be mentally impaired, and Lucy shivered as he placed a hand on her shoulder as she sat by Martin's bedside for the umpteenth day running.

Hugh arrived at that moment. He had been a tower of strength since the accident, calling at the hospital whenever he was in the area, phoning colleagues who were dealing with Martin and passing on to her any snippets of information that he could acquire and she might not. One part of her rejoiced at seeing so much of him, the other part of her dreaded the time when he would announce his plans with Hattie, or simply not be around so much because the need was not there. She was, too, dreading the time when she must pluck up the courage to tell him what she had decided, that she would marry Martin if he wanted her to. It was easy, seeing Martin helpless and apparently alone in the world, to stick to that resolve.

She felt increasingly, as the days passed, the desire to hand over the responsibility for Martin to someone else, or at least share it, but not in the same fashion as she shared the problem with Hugh, but with someone who was personally close to Martin. The trouble was, there didn't seem to be anybody in that category. He had bags of theatrical friends, dozens of whom sent cards and flowers, but no relatives that anyone knew of, and no really close friends, not even, surprisingly thought Lucy, a girlfriend.

When after ten days Martin was allowed other visitors besides Lucy, actor friends drove down from London, or from Chichester where they were in rehearsal at the Festival Theatre, or from Brighton and Southampton, not far away, where they were currently on stage in the various local theatres. They came armed with bottles of wine and boxes of chocolates and theatre gossip, but not one of them was really close to Martin or knew whether he had relatives or not.

The world of theatre was a world on its own, with a shifting population that touched from time to time, but did not adhere, thought Lucy, and was more than ever glad that she had made the more mundane profession of nursing her career.

She would not have been surprised at how heartily Hugh would have endorsed this sentiment, had he known of it. On the occasions that his visits to Martin clashed with those of the theatre fraternity, he was reminded of his feckless wife and the misery she had caused him and their children by her excursions into a society so alien to medicine. Not that all her jet-setting society friends were involved in the world of the theatre, but the butterfly existence that some of them seemed to lead was similar to the make-believe world of Martin Lacey and his friends.

Hugh knew he was unfairly biased, but he was genuinely concerned for Lucy, who he thought might be seduced back into Martin's circle of friends and the career that she had once aspired to. Also, as a doctor and an intelligent man, he could see how vulnerable she was with her kind heart to Martin's present helplessness and need, and with the knowledge of his epilepsy, she might feel more than ever committed to caring for him on a long-term basis. Certainly Martin, in the little while that he had known him before the accident, had made it plain that he was much attracted to Lucy. Of Lucy's feelings in return he couldn't be sure.

The more Hugh saw of Lucy, the more he longed to explain everything to her, repair the damage done by Hattie's sudden arrival on the night of the spoiled supper party at the Gatehouse. He would like to make a fresh start with Lucy, let her know that it was because of her extraordinary beauty, which so reminded him of his ex-wife, that he presented to her his grimmest front to keep her at arm's length.

He knew himself to be naturally reserved, a reserve that he had deliberately fostered to shield himself and his family from further hurt, a reserve that he tended to discard only for his children and his patients. But it was a front, and he was aware that beneath it his true self was capable of loving again with passion and devotion.

He knew for certain now that he was in love with Lucy, and just hoped he hadn't lost her irrevocably to Martin, who, as a sick man, had an unfair advantage over him. An advantage not to be underestimated where someone of Lucy's gentle nature was concerned.

It seemed increasingly to depend on Lucy what happened to Martin when he left hospital. Nobody else seemed to care, or perhaps realise the problems that might have to be faced. His friends were kind enough, most of them were genuine enough, but they spent their days and nights on the stage, or in rehearsal, or searching for parts. They hadn't the wherewithal to offer long-term commitment to Martin or anyone else. They weren't unkind or insensitive, just too busy to be committed.

Because she felt so responsible for him, Lucy was beginning to find her visits to Martin sometimes rather trying. It wasn't that he was a difficult patient — on the contrary, he had taken the news of his epilepsy rather well, and had regained his normal cheerfulness with his return to consciousness. Lucy admired him for that, but she had no idea if he recalled how seriously he had spoken to her about their relationship in those few days before his accident. He hadn't said anything about it as his health improved, but whether that was because he'd forgotten it, or changed his mind, or was being noble because he didn't want her saddled with a partial invalid, she had no idea.

She couldn't decide whether to bring the matter up herself, or let it hang between them, an unresolved problem. Martin treated her with great affection, like an old and valued friend whom he trusted completely. Was it because of this that he asked her to be present when he spoke to the consultant in charge of his case about the prognosis for his future, or because she was a nurse and would understand the jargon, as he put it? Or was it because he had no one else close enough to support him?

Lucy mulled over all these possibilities as the days passed, but reached no conclusions. It was a great temptation to cry off a visit to the hospital when, about a fortnight after the accident, her new car had to go in for its first service. It really wouldn't hurt missing one visit, she reasoned, especially as Martin now had other visitors. Not that they were very dependable, a dozen people might turn up and stay for hours, or a lone acquaintance for a few minutes.

Lucy sighed. If only she didn't feel so responsible for Martin. She would feel guilty as hell if she didn't visit. She decided to ask Hugh if he would take her to the hospital that afternoon. In view of the caring, kindly and unstinting help he'd given, since Martin's admission to hospital, it was odd that she did this with a mixture of emotions, not sure how he would respond.

'Love to,' he said, sounding pleased and surprised. Clearly the last thing he expected was for her to ask him a favour. 'What time shall I pick you up?'

'Two-thirty?'

'Fine, see you then.'

His voice had as always caused her heart and pulses to thump in anticipation. He seems to be in my bloodstream, she thought fancifully, and I can't even think about him without some physical reaction. She felt that every small thing that he had ever said or done was imprinted on her mind for ever.

The rare moments of deep, almost spiritual understanding that had sprung up between them occasionally in the past had not recurred since Martin's accident, neither had the slow build-up of understanding that had seemed about to overtake them on the night that the Blunts' baby had been born. Of course, she herself had been responsible for scuppering that by leaving so hurriedly when Hattie had appeared when she and Hugh were embracing in the Mini.

The regret that she experienced for having driven away that night leaving Hugh upset and angry about Hattie's arrival, and perhaps ready and willing to explain her role in his life, continued to plague her. Well, her father used to tease her about her over-active imagination, and chide her for often acting precipitately. 'Don't go jumping the gun, Lucy, love,' he would say. 'Things aren't always what they seem. Give people a chance to explain themselves.' And her mother, who was a great quoter of proverbs, used to say, 'Look before you leap, darling, look before you leap.'

The more she saw and learned of Hugh as man, father and doctor, the more she admired him, and the more determined she had become about living out her life near him, if this was what circumstances dictated. She didn't quite know how she was going to manage this sort of life, but if she didn't marry Martin, and that was at this moment an unknown quantity, even the thought of the sexy Hattie in charge at the Old Rectory wouldn't make her change her mind.

The accident had confirmed her decision to stay put at the school even if she married Martin. They would make the school and the Gatehouse their main home. Martin's brush with death, had underlined the fact that life was a fragile, ephemeral sort of thing, and one must hang on to the good things even if they weren't perfect. Since coming to this decision, she had reached a kind of peace with herself and hoped that Hugh, who she thought was looking rather drawn of late, would find peace too.

Getting dressed ready for Hugh's arrival at half-past two, she decided to wear the lightweight peat-coloured woollen skirt that she had worn on the day of the accident, and which she hadn't worn since. She couldn't explain why she wanted to wear this skirt on this particular day with its reminders of that fateful morning, unless it was because she knew that Hugh's solid and comforting presence would give her courage. She teamed it with a green and white candy-striped silk shirt unbuttoned at the collar and tucked into the skirt's waistband, with a suede belt and waistcoat over the top.

In deference to the May sunshine she decided to opt for strappy leather, high-heeled sandals over bare feet, aware that they showed off her slim ankles admirably. Letting herself out of the porch door when she heard Hugh sounding the horn of the Range Rover, she realised that this was the first time that she had given a thought about what to wear since Martin had come to grief at the foot of the drive. Was it for Martin, she wondered, or for Hugh that she had taken the trouble to consciously dress to please?

'You look stunning,' he said as he leaned over and closed the passenger door. 'Delicious! Have you dressed for your chauffeur or your patient?' His remark surprised her because it matched her own thoughts, and because she wasn't used to Hugh making such comments and in such a fashion. Words like 'delicious' and 'stunning' didn't come easily to him, she was sure.

She couldn't answer at once, so she smiled vaguely at him while her thoughts churned around.

How was she to answer his question, without giving herself and her feelings for him away, and perhaps unwittingly increasing the tension that hovered so often between them? Maybe he wasn't teasing when he'd asked whom she had dressed for. Suppose he had wanted her to say that it was for him? Suppose he didn't?

Perhaps she could find a middle way, so that no one got hurt, and Hugh had either a face-saver or encouragement depending on what he was looking for. She lowered her lids and tried to look demure. 'Oh, I always try to please all my audience,' she said quietly. 'But I suppose a sick man and an old and close friend must take precedence over my chauffeur, however kind.' She turned on him her full smile and guileless green eyes.

Hugh, who had begun to have faint stirrings of hope for himself in relation to Lucy now that the Martin character was on the mend, got the message like a punch in the solar plexus; she was in love, or at least infatuated with this fantastic-looking chap from her past, this actor type turned director. What more could a woman with one-time aspirations towards the stage want? Hugh felt that the bottom had dropped out of his world, though nothing of this showed in his professionally controlled manner.

'Quite right,' he said, sounding to Lucy's ear, which was sensitive to his every mood, unmoved by her answer. 'The sick need all the help we can give them. Go in there and slay the man. Seeing you looking like this will do more for him than all the medicine in the world, encourage him to get better that much quicker, and that's what you want, Lucy, isn't it, to have him up and about again?' Hugh's grey eyes met hers, without, it seemed to Lucy, a flicker of emotion in them, except for. . .was it, a challenge? A look that dared her to be honest with herself?

'Of course I want him well as soon as possible,' she said stiffly in a rather high voice. 'But I can't expect to work miracles, can I?' She was furious to find tears welling up in her eyes, and her throat getting tight.

'Ah, but you can, Lucy,' said Hugh in an oddly soft,

thick voice. 'That's precisely what you can do for some people, make miracles happen.' He gave a small smile and his eyes lost some of their steel. 'Go and do your best for the invalid.'

Lucy nodded, and swallowed her tears, wondering, not for the first time, if Hugh could read her mind. It was as if he knew what a turmoil she was in, and was giving her encouragement to sort it out, as if whatever she decided was acceptable to him, as long as she got on with it. Was he really bothered about her reaction to Hattie's appearance that night a few short weeks ago, as his note had implied? Was the fact that he looked tired and drawn anything to do with his personal life, as she'd supposed, or just a natural reaction to overworking?

Would it make one iota of difference to him if she continued to live in Millweir or not? Looking at his patrician profile now, unyielding, unreadable, Lucy thought he probably wouldn't notice. He would go on being the impeccably correct doctor and loving father, a respected and even loved figure, totally absorbed by his work and his children, and perhaps Hattie.

Her new-found calm all but deserted her. There seemed little that she could do in relation to Hugh, but she could be a good friend, and perhaps more, to Martin. But should she encourage him and bring matters to a head?

Now that he was out of danger and coming to terms with his epilepsy, she was beginning to wonder if she should go through with the promise she had privately made, to marry him if he survived. She would have to be honest about not being in love with him. If after knowing that he still wanted her to marry him, she would.

A little later, seated in Martin's pleasant little private room, she continued to mull things over, and still felt muddled and unsure of herself. Fortunately Martin seemed not to notice her monosyllabic replies and babbled happily on about the latest production that was in rehearsal. His ebullience went some way to reassuring her. As long as he had his work in the theatre he would be happy. In fact she realised, sitting there listening to him, that telling him that she wasn't in love with him would do little more than dent his ego, but just the same she rather dreaded doing it.

He was still the same old Martin. Whatever he had said, and however genuine his feelings were for her, his true love was the theatre, and all that went with it. He wouldn't compromise on his dream, and she wouldn't compromise on her future. She would either marry him, or remain the hardworking nurse, owner of Mill School, and friend and colleague to Hugh Bellamy and his family, whether Hugh noticed or not. It was really up to Martin.

Well, perhaps something would emerge on the drive back with Hugh that would enlighten her a little. She couldn't stop herself anticipating with pleasure the thought of sitting beside him as they journeyed to Millweir, even if he was the strong, silent, handsome man of fiction.

It wasn't to be, though. She was just about to leave Martin and meet Hugh in the car park as arranged, when he appeared in the doorway of the room. He still looked tired, but there was an alertness about him that had been missing on their drive to town.

He said, without any preamble, 'A patient of mine from the village has been admitted as an emergency. They're a bit short-staffed here and I've volunteered to give a hand in surgery. I do apologise, Lucy, but it's a child I know and I hope my presence will help. I've arranged for a taxi to take you back to Millweir—is that OK?'

'That's kind of you,' she said. 'I do hope the child will be all right. May I ask what's wrong?'

'Abdominal emergency, perf appendix, possibly.' He stared at her in an abstracted fashion. She thought, he's already there, with the child in Theatre, wondering about his chances. 'Good luck,' she whispered as he left the room.

'That guy,' said Martin as the door closed behind Hugh, 'is nuts about you. You should do something about it, put him out of his misery.'

Lucy stared at him open-mouthed. Could the perceptive Martin be right? Had he penetrated the façade that Hugh presented to her? She went red and then white at the prospect. But she mustn't lose control in front of Martin. She swallowed and said sharply, 'Martin, you shyster! Only a few weeks ago you said he was a stuffed shirt and I shouldn't waste my time on him. We weren't suited, if I remember rightly.'

Martin shrugged, but had the grace to blush. His blue eyes looked brighter than ever as he fixed them unwaveringly on her. 'A lot's happened to me since then, poppet. I've got to know him better—he's called in here frequently. That man's got hidden depths. And I've got to know you and myself better too on account of almost meeting up with,' he widened his eyes and made a frightened face, 'the Angel of Death. My God, it certainly puts things in perspective!'

Lucy contrived to look indignant, but she felt that a great load was about to be lifted off her shoulders. 'Martin Lacey,' she said severely, 'are you telling me your near-proposal of marriage is off?'

Martin grinned. 'Thank the lord for that,' he said, sighing with relief. 'You're pleased, Lucy Shaw, aren't you?'

Lucy shook her head, but she couldn't hide from him the fact that she was delighted.

'We wouldn't have suited, Lucy,' he said cheerfully after a moment. 'You're quite fixed on this career of sticking needles in people and stitching up cuts, and looking after this school of yours too, and I'm married to the stage. But I did mean it when I spouted all that serious stuff in the Copper Kettle, and who knows? We might have made it work.'

'Yes,' Lucy agreed with a rather wistful smile, 'we might have made it work.' Just for a moment, the relief of knowing that she didn't have to tell Martin she didn't love him was offset as a wave of desolation swept over her. No Martin, and probably no Hugh, in spite of what Martin had said about him being keen on her, at least not as a life partner, with Hattie on the scene.

Resolutely she pulled herself together as she said her goodbyes to Martin and walked down the long corridor to meet her taxi. 'I don't know what more you want, Lucy Shaw,' she muttered. 'You've got a whole school full of people to care for. One big, happy family, as Isabel Mottram is fond of saying.'

CHAPTER ELEVEN

'THE quacks tell me I'll be fit enough to be discharged next week,' was the news with which Martin greeted Lucy a few days later. 'They're getting me stabilised on something for this epilepsy thing, and all my damaged bits and pieces are well on the mend. They suggest a spot of sunshine for a few weeks, so where shall we go to convalesce, old thing, you and I?'

A typical Martin remark, thought Lucy. The fact that he had withdrawn his offer of marriage, tentative though that had been, didn't prevent him from assuming that they could go off somewhere together.

She said firmly, '*We* won't be going anywhere, Martin. I've got a school to run.'

'Oh, come on, love, you can be spared for a bit. The school doesn't own you — you own it.'

'Same thing, I'm afraid. Ownership brings with it tremendous responsibility — I'd no idea until now.'

'Lucy, you exaggerate. It's not as if you were a highly trained teacher, you employ people to teach. Come on, my darling, be sensible about this.'

They were on the small balcony opening off his room and overlooking a little courtyard. Lucy leant against the balcony rail and looked down at him. He really was handsome, but astonishingly selfish. At this moment he could think only about where he was going to convalesce, and he believed she would drop everything to go with him. She opened her mouth to reinforce her argument against going, but Martin snaked out a hand, grabbed her wrist and pulled her down on to his lap.

'You are mine, wench,' he said with a theatrical

laugh. 'You must do my bidding.' He gave her a smacking kiss.

Lucy freed herself from his grasp. For someone who had been critically ill he was remarkably strong.

'Well,' she said, wriggling from his lap, 'the answer's still no. You'll have to approach one of your other hapless maidens, this one's not up for grabs.'

'Pity,' he sighed heavily. 'What a waste. Are you sure I can't tempt you, sweet Lucy?'

'Positive.'

'Ah, well, it was worth a try. By the way, how are you and your medical man getting along, any developments on that front?'

Lucy shook her head and turned to look out across the courtyard, unwilling for Martin to see the pain in her eyes. She was bitterly disappointed that Hugh hadn't tried to get in touch since operating on the village child. 'I haven't seen anything of him since he drove me here when my car was being serviced.' Martin's eyebrows shot up. And Lucy said defensively, 'He's a busy man, and summer term has just started, so I'm busy too. Just because we live in a small village, it doesn't mean that we live in each other's pockets, you know — or want to.'

'You do if you're two people in love,' replied Martin solemnly. 'Lucy, don't let this Bellamy fellow get away, just because of pride or any other well bred emotion. Go for him. I told you before that he's crazy about you. I don't know what it is that's keeping him from telling you so, but it's a fact.'

Lucy couldn't keep her defences up any longer. Here was someone she could talk to, who had divined how she felt about Hugh, and seemed sure how Hugh felt about her. And she knew that Martin, for all his pretending, could be kind and helpful.

'He has commitments elsewhere,' she said quietly.

'He's not free, even if you're right and he does love me.'

'Rubbish. He's divorced, isn't he?'

'Yes.'

'Then what's the problem? There's no doubt about him being in love with you, it's as plain as a pikestaff. To me it was obvious that first day that I met you together. It was quite a challenge, trying to give him a run for his money.'

'Martin,' Lucy didn't know whether to be angry or amused, 'do you mean to say that you only went after me to spite Hugh?'

'No, old thing, not just because of that, although it's what started me off. I simply fell for you all over again, and I truly thought that Hugh was not for you. I'd only seen his holier-than-thou front, not what's underneath. I told you the other day, being ill has made me appreciate that man's worth. But he sure keeps it well hidden.'

'Yes, he does.' Lucy swallowed more threatening tears. 'And there have been moments when I thought he was in love with me, or beginning to be, but something always happened to spoil them. I know he was badly hurt by his ex-wife. It seems to have made him very hard.'

Martin shook his head. 'Not hard, just hiding behind a mask. He's pretending all the time. Acting, Lucy, and that's something I know about. But he's not beyond help,' he grinned boyishly. 'And you're the maiden to go to the rescue.'

'It's not as simple as that. There's Hattie.'

'Who the hell's Hattie?'

Lucy did her best to explain the mysterious Hattie.

'I can't see your precious Dr Bellamy playing fast and loose with anyone, least of all someone who might jeopardise his kids and his career. I bet there's a perfectly simple explanation for her presence, like there always is in the best farces. Why don't you simply ask him about her?'

'Yes, that's what I had planned to do once, but something stopped me.' She smiled. She was beginning to feel better.

'As it always does in the best tradition of a farce. Only in the last moments of the last act does all become clear. Now tell me, lovely Lucy, what comes first, life or acting?'

'You mean all the world being a stage and all the people, et cetera?

'Precisely.' He stood up and put his hands on her shoulders and shook her gently. 'Lucy, go back to your little village now, and make things happen between you and Bellamy. He's stiff-backed with pride, though for good reason. Go and bend him a bit, for both your sakes.' He kissed her on both cheeks and gave her a little push. 'Go on—exit stage right,' he said.

Her mind in a whirl, Lucy drove home through the early evening sunshine. She felt lighter and happier than she had for weeks. Martin had put things in perspective. She held her future, and Hugh's, in her hands. At least it was within her power to untangle the web of misunderstanding that existed between them, by bringing it into the open, even if it did not come out as she wanted it to. She was not as sure as Martin that Hattie played an innocent role in the Bellamy household, but at least with courage she could straighten things out.

She didn't lack this courage, it was just a question of sorting out how and when she should tackle Hugh, to get their lives sorted out. Talking about confronting the man you loved and insisting that he told you that he loves you, was one thing; doing it another. It was going to take time and perhaps some manipulating before Hugh could be brought to the right frame of mind.

Martin's flair for sizing up a romantic situation was a comfort because it was so convincing, and anyway it confirmed what her heart had been telling her for some time, not only that she was in love with Hugh, but that he was in love with her. The attraction had been there from the beginning and compounded over their many meetings, but what had prevented either one of them from being honest? He, presumably, because of Hattie.

'And you, Lucy,' she asked herself, 'why didn't you come clean and admit your love for Hugh?' She answered herself. 'Because I felt at first that he didn't love me, and then that he was responsible for somebody else, and I was responsible for his children's schooling, and somehow it would have been dishonourable to have in any way jeopardised that by giving in to my feelings. And I was, still am, scared of loving a mature man with a family.' That, she decided as she at last slipped into the lanes a few miles from home, was what still bothered her. She was afraid Hugh wouldn't take her love seriously. Could she make him believe it was the real thing?

Over the months she had heard all sorts of rumours, about Hugh's life with his ex-wife. She was very beautiful, stunning, wagging tongues had informed her, but quite unsuitable as a mother and wife, particularly to a medical man. Angela de Winter had said that it was a miracle and only Hugh's self-control that had kept the threads of their marriage together for so long.

'She was an absolute tramp,' Angela, not usually vindictive or gossipy, had said. 'Poor Hugh, I think he'd have ditched her long ago had it not been for the children and his work, both of which had to be protected. I think it's made him wary of women in general, and beautiful women in particular.'

'I can understand that,' Lucy had replied. No wonder

Hugh was a man apart and so many women fell for him; the fact that he seemed unobtainable must add to his attraction.

Perhaps that was where Hattie came in; perhaps she found him irresistible because of his remoteness. But why had Hugh responded to her with such an easy yet irritated affection that night? It was the sort of familiarity that existed only between married people or those very close. And Hattie was very beautiful in her wild sort of way, so why wasn't Hugh scared of a relationship with her? She must be very special indeed.

All these thoughts and more occupied Lucy as she drove home from the hospital. She was bolstered up by Martin's conviction that Hugh loved her and that it was up to her to set the ball of fate rolling. She would do that and confront this enigmatic man who held her heart in his hands. She would be honest with him, and pray that he would be honest in return.

On this resolution, she turned between the pillars at the entrance to the school drive. They still showed the scars of Martin's collision with them weeks earlier. A van was coming down the centre of the drive quite fast, the driver seeming oblivious to Lucy's approaching Mini, so that she had to swerve dramatically to avoid the oncoming vehicle. She missed it by a fraction, and slithered on to the wet grass verge, coming to a halt just before meeting the hedge.

The van pulled up and the driver shouted through his open window, 'You all right, darlin'?'

Lucy waved a hand to show that she was alive and kicking, and the van disappeared through the gates. She sat and gathered herself together, head bent over the driving wheel as she recovered from her close encounter. She was sure she wouldn't have been so shocked had it not been for the recent accident, but while she sat with bent head she thought about the quite sharp bend into the drive from the lane and decided that something would have to be done about it. The pillars were waiting to be repaired; she might as well have them removed, and the drive widened while she was about it.

She felt pleased with herself for having made the first truly original decision about Mill School, apart from the introduction of drama, since her arrival. She knew it was a good idea and one that she would implement as soon as possible. She couldn't think why nobody had suggested it before, especially the minibus driver. It must be hell manipulating a large vehicle through that gateway.

Just at that moment another large vehicle rounded the bend from the lane, and she raised her head just in time to see, in her driving mirror, Hugh's Range Rover turn into the drive.

She panicked. I can't speak to him now, I'm not ready. She buried her head in her arms draped over the steering-wheel.

He shot to a halt beside her and leapt out of his car. 'Lucy, my darling, are you all right?' He was standing by the Mini fiddling with the door handle. 'Lucy, please speak to me.' He succeeded in opening the door.

Lucy, red-faced and embarrassed, looked up at him. 'I'm fine, Hugh, fine. Somebody came down the drive fast and I had to swerve to avoid them, but nothing happened. I was just sitting here thinking.' She sat up very straight and looked at him truculently as if expecting that he would argue. 'I'm going to have the entrance widened. No wonder poor Martin nearly died as he was trying to turn in, not realising about the sharp bend.'

Hugh leaned against the side of the Mini. He looked pale. 'Yes, of course,' he said tonelessly, 'Martin.' He backed towards the Range Rover standing with the driver's door wide open as he had left it in his hurry to reach Lucy. He rested his buttocks against the high seat.

Lucy scrambled out of her car. 'Hugh, are you all right?' He looked white as a sheet.

'Fine,' he mumbled. 'Just shocked. I thought you. . .'

'What shall I do? How can I help? Oh, Hugh, darling, please tell me — you look awful. I'm frightened, dearest, darling Hugh, what shall I do?' Her voice soared, but she couldn't help it. She thought she had never been as frightened in her life as now, seeing the man she loved above all else looking so stricken, looking as if he was going to die. All her nursing training seemed momentarily to have deserted her, and she felt as ignorant as any layman confronted with a medical emergency.

He managed a grin of sorts. 'I'm only a bit faint,' he said. He ducked his head down between his knees. 'Be all right in a jiff.' When he raised his head he had a little more colour in his cheeks, and his eyes, clouded before, looked bright again and in focus.

Lucy crouched beside him and chafed at his cold hands, her small paws massaging his large ones gently, lovingly.

'Did you mean that?' he said softly after a moment. 'Dearest and darling — you weren't just being — well, theatrical?'

'Oh, Hugh, I wouldn't dream of pretending with you.' She bent her head for a moment and then raised it and looked straight into his eyes. 'I love you, Hugh. I have done for months. But I didn't know, I wasn't sure. . .'

Hugh breathed in deeply and raised himself to his full height and gently pulled her up beside him.

'Oh, Lucy, dear lovely Lucy. What a pair of idiots we've been! But I thought. . . Look, we can't stay here. I've got to get up to the school to look at a child who's had a fall. Ruth phoned me just now. And no, my darling, she's not badly hurt, so don't open those great green eyes of yours in horror.' He grinned like a schoolboy and bent to kiss her very casually on the lips. 'Now you go into your exquisite little cottage and make a pot of strong tea and wait for me to get back from the san. I'll not be long, I promise you, my love, and then we'll talk and get everything straightened out. We've a hell of a lot to sort out, you and I.'

CHAPTER TWELVE

WHEN Hugh returned, his usual calm had deserted him. 'My heart nearly stopped,' he said, 'when I thought you were hurt, or even worse.' He still looked very pale.

They faced each other in the hall. There was utter silence as their eyes feasted on each other, then Hugh opened his arms, and Lucy went into them, knowing this was where she belonged.

He brushed little butterfly kisses all over her face and neck, then fastened his lips on hers, at first gently and then with ever-demanding passion. Her mouth opened to the probing of his tongue as they stood locked together, his hands caressing her back and stroking her buttocks as he strained her against him, thighs touching, and she felt the hardness of his desire.

He lifted his head for a moment and groaned, 'Lucy, it's been so long. I want you, my love, I'm desperate for you.'

'And I you,' she mumbled. 'So badly. But Hugh,' she forced herself to ease back a fraction from him, 'we must talk first.'

'Talk? What, now, my darling?' His hoarse voice sounded baffled. His eyes were dark with passion, but he slackened the pressure of his hands on the soft roundness of her bottom, took a few deep breaths, and in an almost normal voice said, 'Of course, I'm rushing you, my dearest girl—forgive me.'

Lucy shook her head. 'No, Hugh, it's not that. I want to make love too. You're not rushing me, but there is something that you have to tell me, then everything will be perfect.'

'Anything.' He cupped her face with his long, strong fingers. His thumbs traced over her chin and lips.

She had to force herself to ignore his touch and the longing to return it that overwhelmed her. She said in a whisper, 'I want to know about Hattie. Everything, Hugh.'

He stared. 'But you know about Hattie. I explained in the note I sent the day after our spoilt supper party.'

'No, you didn't, you said you *would* explain about Hattie.'

He smiled gently at her. 'Of course, I remember — I decided to tell you in person, and the note was scribbled in a hurry as I was on my way out on an emergency call. Have you been worrying all this time, my love, about Hattie?'

Lucy nodded. 'Yes,' she whispered.

'Oh, my dearest.' He kissed her gently and nuzzled her neck.

In spite of her happiness and Hugh's arms still about her, she couldn't keep a trace of bitterness, or was it fear, out of her voice. 'So for goodness' sake tell me about her, so I can lay her ghost for ever.'

Her vehemence surprised Hugh. He said softly. 'My dear, there's nothing to tell. Hattie's my sister — well, my stepsister.' He grinned broadly, and rubbed his nose against hers. 'Why, my love, who did you think she was?'

'Your lover, or mistress or something.'

Hugh rocked with laughter, and then seeing her hurt expression, took her hands in his, brought them to his lips, and kept them clasped just below her chin. 'Dearest Lucy, I don't go in for such exotica. Mistress indeed.'

'But she — you — she didn't sound like a sister that night.'

Hugh sighed. 'Hattie doesn't sound like any man's

sister,' he said ruefully. 'She adopted this role of *femme fatale* as a teenager and has improved on it since.'

Lucy stared at him. 'Are you sure she thinks of you as only a brother?'

He was surprised momentarily, then laughed. 'She fancied me briefly when she knew I wasn't her natural brother, but it was the hero-worship a younger child often gives to an older sibling. She soon got over it. She's man-mad in a rather immature, innocent way, in spite of a superficial sophistication, and she tends to get into fixes and has to be untangled.'

'And you do the untangling?'

'Yes. When our parents died she was seven, I seventeen. We were looked after by caring relatives, but she looked to me for affection. And that, dear love, is all there is to it. Brotherly love. I wish she'd meet the right man and settle down, but it doesn't look like it at present, and as long as she needs me, I have to be around. And her home is mine wherever that is. Will you mind, my love?'

Lucy's tender heart was bruised by the story of a brother and sister thrown together after a mutual tragedy.

'Of course I won't mind. No wonder I liked her, though I couldn't imagine why, when I thought she meant something very special to you in a romantic way.'

The months following that May evening were happy for Lucy. Hugh loved her very much and didn't mind showing it.

'I love you to distraction,' he said, 'forever and a day, and all that romantic nonsense that the songs rave about.' He took her into his arms and kissed her with breathtaking passion, so that her lips felt sore and bruised and her chest ached because she couldn't breathe properly.

On the occasion that he made this over-the-top declaration, they were standing in the gracious little hall of the Gatehouse, which was filled with the autumnal sunshine of a September evening. Hugh had arrived unexpectedly.

'You're supposed to be at the University Hospital,' said Lucy, drawing back from him and heading for the kitchen.

'But aren't you pleased, my darling, that I managed to get away early, and came flying to your side?' His grey eyes, once so arctic, were twinkling with a teasing humour.

'Of course I am. Every moment with you is a bonus.'

'You mean that? I often have this little twinge of fear that I'll arrive back from an emergency and find the handsome Martin Lacey kneeling at your feet.'

'Idiot. You know anything there was between Martin and me was finished yonks ago. In fact, if he hadn't convinced me that you were mad for me—drooling, he said—I might never have given you a second look,' she teased back.

Finding that they had both got this quirky, dry humour was a bonus on top of all the other delicious secrets they were discovering about each other.

Lucy and Hugh kept their feelings at bay when they were with his children, who happily accepted Lucy's more frequent visits to their home as their friendship, without, apparently, considering that anything romantic existed between them.

They were discreet at all times. They had to be, given the background of a conservative, gossip-hungry village, and patients, staff and pupils, to whom they each represented authority—though their staff must have been aware of their changing relationship.

They didn't mind the necessary discretion, and as long as they would be able to persuade the Bellamy children to accept Lucy as a stepmother, they were happy with their low-key relationship.

As Hugh said, 'It's all rather Victorian, like conducting an old-fashioned courtship under the eye of a chaperon, frustrating at times but worth it for the end result.'

On the first occasion that they were able to make love, when Hugh's presence in the house might be considered as an innocent professional meeting, it was a tender, passionate, overwhelmingly exciting joining together such as neither had experienced before. Subsequent occasions had been just as satisfying, sometimes wildly passionate and lustful, at others gentle and lingering.

But tonight Lucy sensed that he had rushed back from the university not to make love, but to talk.

'Darling, go and pour us both a sherry while I get something ready to eat,' she suggested. 'An omelette and salad all right?'

'Fine.'

He brought the sherry into the kitchen and watched her beating eggs. He was thoughtful, but not unhappy. The salad was already tossed, looking an attractive abstract of pale greens and reds in a wooden bowl. Idly Hugh turned it over before serving it on to the waiting plates as the omelettes sizzled in the frying-pan.

Not until they had toasted each other by raising their glasses of sherry, smiled, and leaned across the small kitchen table to kiss, did he speak.

'About the wedding, my dearest, I think we should begin to make plans and dates.' He sounded a little pompous.

'I'm ready any time, Lord and Master,' said Lucy, smiling at his pomposity. 'You have but to say the word. But I thought we were giving the children a bit longer to get used to the idea.'

'I think they're quite ready, and we should tell them of our intentions as soon as possible.'

'Why not, if you think the children. . .' Her voice trailed off in a tremble of uncertainty.

'Lucy, the children love you.'

'Yes, as a nurse, your friend, but as your wife, their future stepmother?' Suddenly she was apprehensive. She leaned both elbows on the table and rested her chin on her hands to stop them shaking. 'Why the sudden rush, Hugh? Why are you so on edge?'

He stood up jerkily and jangled the change in his pocket. 'You'll never believe what I'm going to tell you.'

'Try me, darling.' Her heart thumped uncomfortably.

He cleared his throat. 'It's particularly awkward because I'm a man of science and don't believe in such rubbish.'

She asked patiently, 'What rubbish?'

'Fortune-telling by stars, and palm-reading and so on.'

'I wouldn't expect you to. It may surprise you, my love, to find that a hell of a lot of unscientific people don't either.'

He flushed beneath the summer tan that still held, and looked sheepish. 'Sorry, I must sound unbearably priggish.'

'Not a bit,' she grinned. 'Oh, Hugh, you are a darling.'

'Forgiven?' he asked, leaning across to kiss her.

'Forgiven.'

He became suddenly brisk. 'At the hospital today, I met the aunt of the little girl who hadn't spoken for a long time. She was grateful for what she thought I'd done for her niece, and offered to read my palm as a sort of. . .present. She was so honest and earnest, thinking she was doing me a favour, that I couldn't refuse. Anyway, the upshot of it was that she virtually repeated our history—how we met, it was raining, we had tea, and so on. It was uncanny. I wanted to disbelieve it. Damn it, I do disbelieve it, but. . .but she went on to say that I should marry the lady I'd met on that rainy day, as soon as possible, or words to that effect.'

He looked so forlorn and bewildered. Clearly nothing like this had ever happened to him before, this feeling that one's affairs were in someone else's hands.

Lucy didn't believe in palm-reading either, but she was less fazed by it. She got up and moved round the table. 'Come on, love, let's have coffee in the parlour and talk this through.'

Hugh didn't move. 'That's not all,' he said tonelessly after a moment. 'When I got home, being early, I decided to do a bit of paperwork before coming to see you. I opened the French doors of the surgery to the garden, and guess what?'

Lucy shook her head. 'I'm fresh out of ideas.'

'The twins were sitting outside and discussing *us*.'

She licked her dry lips and whispered, 'Hugh, they don't hate me, do they?'

Hugh's face, so near her own, registered total surprise. 'Hate you? They love you, they think we ought to get together as soon as possible, that's what I overheard them saying.'

'You're having me on!'

'Darling, I kid you not. Can you imagine how I felt, hearing that after having *my palm read* by a sort of out-of-season performer at the end of the pier?'

'Bewildered?'

'You bet.'

'So, on account of a palmist in whom you naturally don't believe, and the immature ramblings of two small children, you feel we should rush into matrimony?'

Hugh took a deep breath. 'Well, love,' he smiled at

her and then kissed her soundly, 'I have to admit to being somewhat jolted by these goings-on, but you know, it's not a bad idea.'

'What about Tess? Will she approve?'

'Ah, Tess. I have to admit that I don't know about Tess. But she's such a sensible and loving child, and she thinks so much of you, Lucy.'

'Yes, I think she does.' Lucy remembered the morning at the end of term when Tess had handed her Hugh's note, and looked as if she approved of her father writing to her drama teacher. 'Let's go over to the Old Rectory now, and talk to the children.'

For a moment she thought Hugh was going to refuse to do anything quite so spontaneous, so strong was his conservative, rational approach to everything, including his children, but he didn't. 'Yes, good idea.' He kissed her soundly. 'Let's go.'

They drove round the Green as dusk deepened to twilight and the orange globes of the street-lights hanging between the trees sparkled into life.

A soft breeze sprang up as they turned into the drive of the Old Rectory, and when they got out of the Range Rover, a swirl of red-gold leaves from the Virginia creeper that clothed the walls circled around them.

'Catch the leaves,' called a voice from above, and they saw Tess leaning out of her bedroom window, silhouetted against the light. 'Leaves are good luck, Hattie said.' She peered down at them, laughing, happy, seeming to wish them well. 'Leaves are dreams,' she said.

Lucy clutched at a handful of leaves as they drifted past. 'Yes,' she said softly to Hugh, 'a handful of dreams.'

Hugh put strong arms around her and called up to his daughter, 'I've got my dream here, Tess—do you understand?'

'What do you think I am, Daddy, s-stupid and s-stuttering?'

'Oh, Tess,' said her father, 'you're wonderful.' His arms tightened round Lucy. 'And so are you, my darling,' he said in his deep, gravelly voice.

Lucy crushed the rosy leaves in her hand. 'A handful of dreams to last forever,' she said softly, and raised her face to Hugh so he could kiss her.

They were married in November in the school chapel.

Faint sunshine penetrated the mist that hung everywhere. It was meant to be a small wedding with only family present, but, in the event, all the school and half the village were there.

'I suppose you might call them our extended family,' whispered Hugh to Lucy as they stood in the porch, while Piers, as official photographer, manipulated his newly acquired video camera, panning over the group. He zoomed in on his father, tall and distinguised as always, in traditional grey, with a grey topper tucked under one arm while his other encircled his wife's waist.

Piers then trained his camera on his new stepmother, who was wearing a pinky-brownish velvet dress, long, almost to her ankles, with gold embroidery, and a little cap on her head with a short, bouncy veil springing from it. Then he looked at his sisters through his viewfinder, and decided that they looked brilliant, in shimmery blue dresses and with flowers in their hair. Old Dr Hubbard stood beside Lucy; he had given her away. 'Like a father,' Daddy explained. Uncle Clive was best man and stood beside Daddy.

'OK,' called Piers, 'will everybody smile, please?'

And they did.

Mills & Boon

— MEDICAL ROMANCE —

The books for enjoyment this month are:

A BORDER PRACTICE Drusilla Douglas
A SONG FOR DR ROSE Margaret Holt
THE LAST EDEN Marion Lennox
HANDFUL OF DREAMS Margaret O'Neill

♥ ♥ ♥ ♥ ♥

Treats in store!

Watch next month for the following absorbing stories:

JUST WHAT THE DOCTOR ORDERED Caroline Anderson
LABOUR OF LOVE Janet Ferguson
THE FAITHFUL TYPE Elizabeth Harrison
A CERTAIN HUNGER Stella Whitelaw

Available from W.H. Smith, John Menzies, Martins, Forbuoys, most supermarkets and other paperback stockists.

Also available from Mills & Boon Reader Service, Freepost, P.O. Box 236, Thornton Road, Croydon, Surrey CR9 9EL.

Readers in South Africa - write to:
Book Services International Ltd, P.O. Box 41654, Craighall, Transvaal 2024.

EXPERIENCE THE EXOTIC

VISIT . . . INDONESIA, TUNISIA, EGYPT AND MEXICO . . . THIS SUMMER

Enjoy the experience of exotic countries with our Holiday Romance Pack

Four exciting new romances by favourite Mills & Boon authors.

Available from July 1993   Price: £7.20

Mills & Boon

Available from W.H. Smith, John Menzies, Martins, Forbuoys, most supermarkets and other paperback stockists. Also available from Mills & Boon Reader Service, FREEPOST, PO Box 236, Thornton Road, Croydon, Surrey CR9 9EL. (UK Postage & Packaging free)

The truth often hurts...

Sometimes it heals

Critically injured in a car accident, Liz Danvers insists her family read the secret diaries she has kept for years – revealing a lifetime of courage, sacrifice and a great love. Liz knew the truth would be painful for her daughter Sage to face, as the diaries would finally explain the agonising choices that have so embittered her most cherished child.

Available now priced £4.99

WORLDWIDE

Available from W.H. Smith, John Menzies, Martins, Forbuoys, most supermarkets and other paperback stockists.

Also available from Mills and Boon Reader Service, Freepost, P.O. Box 236, Thornton Road, Croydon, Surrey CR9 9EL

Discover the thrill of 4 exciting Medical Romances - FREE

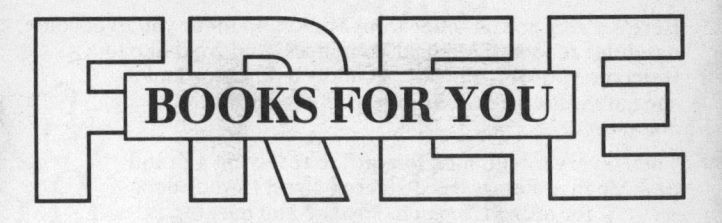

FREE BOOKS FOR YOU

In the exciting world of modern medicine, the emotions of true love acquire an added poignancy. Now you can experience these gripping stories of passion and pain, heartbreak and happiness - with Mills & Boon absolutely FREE! AND look forward to a regular supply of Medical Romances delivered direct to your door.

🌹 🌹 🌹

Turn the page for details of how to claim 4 FREE books AND 2 FREE gifts!

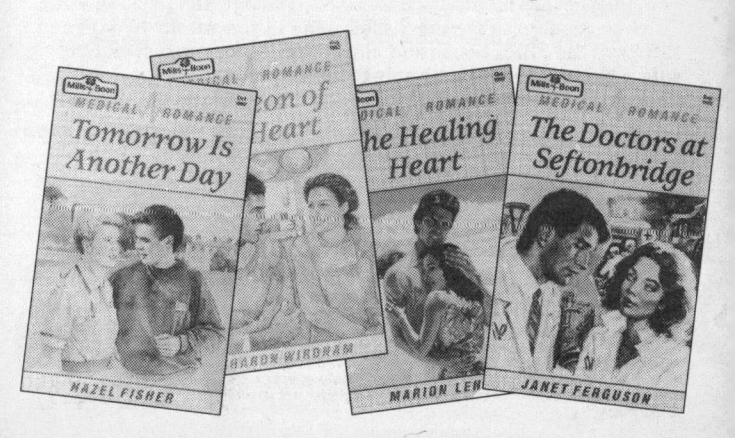

An irresistible offer from Mills & Boon

Here's a very special offer from Mills & Boon for you to become a regular reader of Medical Romances. And we'd like to welcome you with 4 books, a cuddly teddy bear and a special mystery gift - absolutely FREE and without obligation!

Then, every month look forward to receiving 4 brand new Medical Romances delivered direct to your door for only £1.70 each. Postage and packing is FREE! Plus a FREE Newsletter featuring authors, competitions, special offers and lots more...

This invitation comes with no strings attached. You may cancel or suspend your subscription at any time and still keep your FREE books and gifts.

It's so easy. Send no money now but simply complete the coupon below and return it today to:

Mills & Boon Reader Service, FREEPOST, PO Box 236, Croydon, Surrey CR9 9EL.

NO STAMP NEEDED

YES! Please rush me 4 FREE Medical Romances and 2 FREE gifts! Please also reserve me a Reader Service subscription. If I decide to subscribe, I can look forward to receiving 4 brand new Medical Romances every month for only £6.80 - postage and packing FREE. If I choose not to subscribe, I shall write to you within 10 days and still keep the FREE books and gifts. I may cancel or suspend my subscription at any time simply be writing to you.
I am over 18 years of age.   Please write in BLOCK CAPITALS

Ms/Mrs/Miss/Mr _____   EP54D

Address _____

_____

_____ Postcode _____

Signature _____

Offer closes 31st July 1993. The right is reserved to refuse an application and change the terms of this offer. One application per household. Overseas readers please write for details. Southern Africa write to B.S.I. Ltd., Box 41654, Craighall, Transvaal 2024. You may be mailed with offers from other reputable companies as a result of this application. Please tick box if you would prefer not to receive such offers ☐

mps MAILING PREFERENCE SERVICE